Summer of the Greater Yellowlegs

Patrick O'Flaherty

BREAKWATER

Canadian Cataloguing in Publication Data

O'Flaherty, Patrick, 1939 —
    Summer of the greater yellowlegs and other stories

ISBN 0-920911-25-0

I. Title.

PS8579.F52S85 1987   C813'.54   C87-093405-8
PR9199.3.042S85 1987

Drawings, on cover and throughout text, by Angela King-Harris.

The incidents and characters in this book are fictional. Any resemblance to persons living or dead is purely coincidental.

The Publisher gratefully acknowledges the support of The Canada Council.

The Publisher acknowledges the financial contribution of the Cultural Affairs Division of the Department of Culture, Recreation and Youth, Government of Newfoundland and Labrador which has helped make this publication possible.

Contents

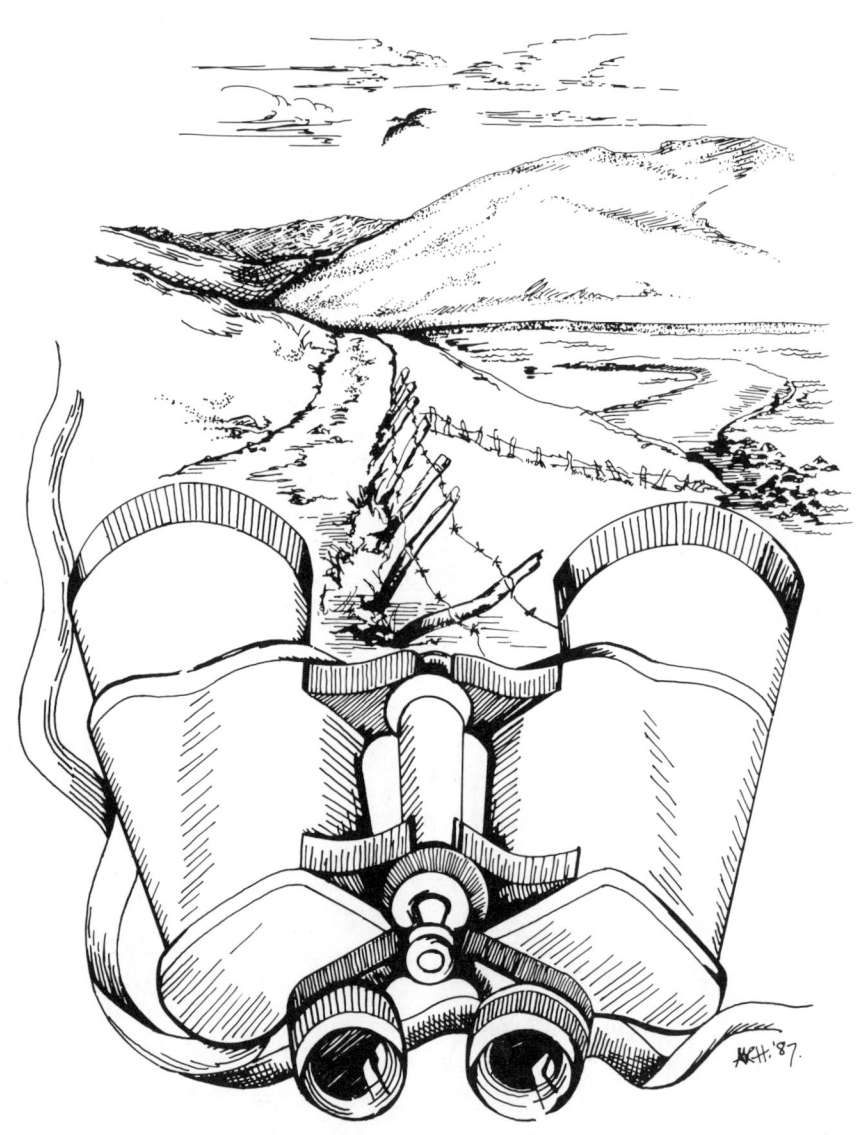

Summer of the greater yellowlegs

He always wondered why people did it. Where did they get the nerve for the final catastrophic placing of the gun barrel in the mouth, the kicking away of the chair? Was betrayal of love a sufficient cause? The long, bleak spring gave him an answer. There could be worse betrayals than those of love. Those of the self were worse. What he had done was an offence against his secret idea of what he was. It wasn't just that his pride was hurt. Let that go; good riddance to that. But the hidden garden inside where the shoots of his life were planted — that had to be protected. To destroy that was death.

In June he retreated from the city to his cabin in Ochre Pit Cove to lick his wounds. On the fourth day of his bitter summer sojourn, he heard the song of the bird.

Having decided that labour would dull pain, he set about putting a new fence around his property, with the help of a muscular and blessedly taciturn fellow from down the shore who didn't object to his brooding silence. The land was of little value and probably wasn't worth the expense of fencing it, especially since there was so much — about seven acres of marsh and rock. "Fence enough for your house and barn, and let the rest go to commons," one of his neighbours advised him last year. But he fenced it all anyway, useless as it was. He lugged the heavy spruce stakes from the barn on his shoulders, two at a time, to the boundaries of his land, walking through bog and over rocky ground, stumbling, falling. The knots on the stakes cut his shoulders and hands, and even rubbed his cheeks raw. What of it! Standing on a barrel, he drove the stakes into the ground with a ten pound maul until bladders appeared and burst on the palms of his hands and his back and legs ached. When his hands could take it no longer, he held the stakes in place for his helper. The maul came crashing down again and again a foot or so from his head. What of that! He stapled fence wire to the stakes and spans, hitting his thumb and fingers with the hammer, tearing a fingernail. He lifted, pulled, stretched, twisted and untwisted wire, scratching his hands, thighs, and arms. No matter! When the helper took an early break, he rolled up the old wire and collected the rotting stakes into piles to be cut later into junks for burning. Amidst this toil, the song came to him in mid-morning. It was a triple, liquid note, sounded from afar, a song he hadn't heard before on this bleak shore where only common breeds and scavengers seemed to thrive. Looking up, he at first couldn't see the bird. Was he hearing things? Yes, there it was. If he took his eye off it for a split second, he lost sight of it. It wheeled above at three or four hundred feet, whistling and heaving in the wind, wisely keeping its distance from treacherous humankind. Watching it make great circles over the cove, he wondered about its mysterious purpose. A noisy bird, he thought, a fearful, insistent, vulnerable, sorrowing bird.

On the seventh day, his fencing finished, seeking more labour, he walked from his cabin inland to Outside Union Pond, on overgrown paths through rough country. The alder bushes were so thick that he lost his way twice and had to climb tolts to get his bearings. The walk took a full two hours. Standing on galled feet and looking at the small pond he had once loved to fish in, he remembered his brother Colin. Twenty-five years ago the two young men stood at the side of the pond, and Colin made his dreadful announcement: "I want to die." Shocked and dismayed, he tried to reason with him, pointing to the possibilities that lay ahead, the pleasures of being alive. "You're not listening, you don't understand," Colin repeated, "I want to die." And the truth was, he didn't understand. Not to care about living, breathing! That was beyond him, then. He hadn't returned to Outside Union Pond until this summer.

The passing of a quarter century had made the memory of his brother no less painful. Why couldn't he be free of it? Grief shouldn't last so long. Staring at the dull, muddy water, where not a trout breached or insect moved, and at the surrounding empty, treeless wilderness, he thought he would never be forgiven for his part in the tragedy. For he had played a part in it, especially in the year that he and his brother attended boarding school together at St. Bonaventure's College. Neither of them had been to St. John's before; he was fifteen, Colin seventeen. They were lonely, and at first had relied on one another, as brothers should. But they drifted apart. Within a month, Colin was getting into trouble with the Christian Brothers. Rebellious, stubborn, a born upstart, he simply declined to follow their stupid rules. Now his heart churned with sickened loathing and rage as he remembered Colin's treatment at the hands of the Brothers. The Protestant Reformation hadn't lasted long enough, he decided. Not enough monasteries had been razed to the ground. Much useful work remained to be done with wrecking balls and bulldozers.

The year had been a battle and Colin, at the end, had become an isolated figure. But he, at least, should have gone to his brother and said he cared. He knew even then, as a child, that he should have done it; he did care, and saw what was happening. But he did nothing. Instead, he kept his distance, seeking friendships with boys. And yet Colin had taken his part more than once in the jungle of boarders' life at the school. Slight in build, he was still a savage fighter with his fists when aroused. Not a few outport bullies, feared by others, wilted before Colin's baleful stare in the common room and, seeing what they had to tackle, walked away.

Tears of anguish rolled down his face and fell into the bog at his feet. Colin had known early the pain of fighting alone, had known betrayal. He too had some glimmer of what that meant. "I'm listening now, I understand now, brother," he said, turning away from the pond to begin the dreary walk home.

The bird was flying when he limped back in the late afternoon, having twisted his ankle in a fall against a stump about a mile from home and gashed his arm on a sharp rock as he fell. The song, a quickly uttered *whee-oodle, whee-oodle, whee-oodle*, seemed to be louder than when he listened earlier and he found it easier to locate the bird even against the darkening sky. He lay on the grass in front of the cabin and contemplated the bird. Its flight was not the idle soaring of a gull or the frantic flapping of a crow; it was fast, easy, fluid, rolling, full of grace and power. Looking for distinctive marks, he saw the legs trailing behind and the long bill and neck. A bittern? Surely not, with that song. When he inquired one day of a passer-by about the kind of bird this was, he was told: "A curlew, maybe." But the curlew, once abundant in Newfoundland, had been killed in such numbers by settlers that it was thought to be extinct on the island. What many mistook for the curlew was the common loon, and even the loon population was on the decline. This was no curlew. Nor was it a chicken hawk or snipe, two suggestions of his rustic fencing companion. A godwit? He understood the species was virtually extinct in North America. This was a bird of the upper atmosphere, an ethereal bird. As he watched and listened, suddenly it came down over the little community and he lost sight of it in the dim twilight. The song ceased. Had it returned to its nest?

Yes, he knew at last what Colin must also have known so early in his life. His life had bottomed out to the sour dregs. Could he stomach what lay ahead, the ignominy, sense of loss, burden of memory? Here there was no light. He had no strength left; he was prostrate on the ground. "I have been half in love with easeful Death," the poet had written. Colin had been an upstart who had weakened and failed. The upstart streak was in his blood too. What would lead him back from the edge? He had no belief left in a spiritual world, but something made him wish for a sign.

Identification of the bird turned out to be a problem too great for local observers, and his neighbours were in any case beginning to eye him warily as he approached with more ornithological questioning. In July he reluctantly drove to the city and came back with a set of binoculars and Peters's *Birds of Newfoundland*. On his return, the postmaster told him that the bird, now the talk of the village, had not been seen in his absence; but when he drove up the lane in his jeep, there it was again, high overhead, though not as high as on previous days, circling directly above his land. With his new binoculars he caught a flash of yellow in the bright sunlight. The book was consulted. Wing span and body size were estimated. The bird was a greater yellowlegs! He had never before seen one. It was said to be found elsewhere on the island, breeding around inland ponds and bogs, but rarely near settlements. Further inquiry established that the species, once known locally as twillicks, had been common along the coast three or four decades ago, but it too had been killed off. An aged neighbour hadn't seen one for "about twenty or thirty years, sir."

Twenty-two years ago, Colin's broken spirit had foundered and he had taken his inevitable path. When they took his body down, they found the scars and lacerations where he had, over time, mutilated himself in many places. Just as he too was cut now, he thought, looking down at his own scratched hands and arms. One deep cut on his wrist still bled a little. He touched it tenderly. It needed looking after.

In the late afternoon, he watched the beautiful greater yellowlegs swerve, sing, and play above his stricken head. Wounds, heal! he prayed; fly, my soul! As darkness approached, the bird descended into his well fenced garden.

352 Pennywell

James John O'Grady, halfway through his second canvass of polling division 8, came out of 348 Pennywell Road and marked his sheets: BS, 3 URCH. That meant only a babysitter and three young children were in the house. They were watching cartoons on TV and eating Kentucky fried chicken. In his hurry last week, he had overlooked #348, which was small and somewhat obscured by trees. He would have to come back at a different hour next Tuesday to catch the two adults at home. Turning eastward, he looked gloomily over the number of houses yet to visit on the darkening, wet street. Was he any good at this? he wondered. According to the campaign manager, a good canvasser should be able to tell quickly, by a kind of intuition, how members of a household would vote; but he found it hard to tell, even after a second try. He could spot the voters for the New Democratic Party; they wore beads, or perhaps one earring, and had a Volvo in the driveway. But how could you identify the others? "Watch for the tell-tale signs," experienced hands at headquarters told him: winks, big smiles, strong handshakes, invitations to come inside. Precious few of these were vouchsafed to J.J. O'Grady. He had seen the poll sheets of other workers, and by each address they had pencilled such comments as, "3 Libs, 1 NDP"; "4 PCs, hopeless"; "6 Libs!!" On his own sheets following his first canvass, his totals ran: 2 Libs; 4 NDPs; 17 PCs; 54 doubtful. The campaign manager had not responded well to this survey, and J.J. wondered how he would take the results of the second canvass, which weren't going to be much different from the first. But he knew that so many "doubtful" marks would be of no help on voting day when he had to go to each house with a "Lib" in it and encourage the voter to get out and cast his ballot. He dreaded having to do this, but all workers had been exhorted to "win their poll."

"A case of beer for everyone who wins his poll," the campaign manager said. J.J. didn't drink. The candidate himself, Franklin Critch, didn't drink either. Didn't drink water. That was the joke around headquarters.

Besides, J.J. hadn't really planned on being a canvasser in one of the eighteen polling divisions in St. John's West. He thought of himself more as a policy man, issuing press releases perhaps, or advising on the proper stand the candidate should take on a burning issue of the day. This would have given him a chance to do what he thought he was best at: writing, reflecting. His high school teacher had written "scribe" on his final report card. Before he offered to join Critch's campaign, he fancied himself sitting around in smoky rooms, chatting about strategy and public relations. But PR wasn't a big factor in the campaign, and there was a shortage of poll workers. Out, therefore, J.J. had to go with the other canvassers. Win the poll! he thought bitterly. Some chance! Large heavy flakes of snow were beginning to fall and he felt wetness in his right sock. He needed new shoes. Dorcas would have to go and buy him new shoes. That was that.

Mark this down to experience, he thought. He was cut out for bigger things than the job of carpet-fitter he now held down. All his efforts to get work with the local newspapers had come to naught. Two years of university meant nothing these days. You had to have a degree in journalism, plus experience. "Imagine!" Dorcas said. Well, there was little point in dreaming. He had a wife and son. He thought grimly of Dorcas: fattish, unambitious, but talkative. Talk your ear off. She said to him once, before he got her in trouble, "You want a big job? I've got a big job for you. Look after me for the rest of my life. That's my job offer." Some offer! He probably wouldn't have married her at all if James II hadn't come along. That was Dorcas's name for their son. But James II had come along, and now ruled the small O'Grady household.

Knock, knock, knock. 350 Pennywell had, according to his earlier notes, 3 PCs plus 1 STB (student boarder) who wasn't sure if he should vote in St. John's or in his home riding in Bonavista Bay, two hundred miles away. J.J. couldn't tell how the student was inclined to vote, but in Bonavista Bay you could still find Liberals and there was hope. This second visit might actually be useful. A woman came to the door; he remembered her from last week. Her face dropped when she saw him. "How are you, my son, back again?" she said without enthusiasm. He entered the porch but learned that the student wasn't in. "He went home last Friday, and I haven't laid eyes on him since," said the woman. "Owes me a week's board, too," she added. J.J. was conscious again of the unstable population — made up of transients, renters and unemployed — of this part of St. John's. Maybe he could write a piece on this after the election. He handed the woman a canvasser's card to give to the boarder on his return. "If he comes back at all," she said. J.J. looked over her shoulder through an open door and saw a macaroni casserole on the stove for supper. He left, slipping and hurting his foot on the loose wooden step. Lifting the leg of his pants, he saw blood where the nail had scratched him. "Watch that step," the woman called after him. Somewhere up the street a dog was being beaten; he heard it whimpering.

Mark this down to experience, he thought again. All this would be of benefit when he himself got into politics. He thought of the life that awaited him: jet planes, important phone calls, speeches, House of Commons' secretaries hurrying to do his bidding. That was the job he wanted. Dorcas be damned! "Newfoundland needs new blood in politics," Critch told him when J.J. joined his campaign. The campaign manager, after taking one look at J.J., praised him for "having what it takes to make it in political life." Only Dorcas held back. She thought his name too incendiary for Newfoundland politics. "Religion still matters here," she said, "your name sends out the message that you're Irish Catholic, and all the Prods would vote against you." When the argument heated up, she added: "Change your name to Bill Jones, Frank Smith, or Cat's Ass and I'll campaign for you; but I'll waste no time beating my gums for J.J. O'Grady in St. John's West." But what did she know? J.J. knew that he was smart and well-spoken. He looked the part, too. From a certain angle, his profile resembled John F. Kennedy's. "My handsome man," Dorcas said to him, more than once. If she only knew what he was planning to do in the big Ottawa hotels. "Room for Mr. and Mrs. O'Grady, please," he would say, glancing at the slim, quiet young thing, the devil in bed, that stood by his side.

"Certainly, Mr. O'Grady," the receptionist would answer; adding, "Will the suite you had last week be satisfactory?"

"Yes, it'll be just fine," replied the rising Member of Parliament.

352 Pennywell. Knock, knock. Consulting his sheet, he saw that last week #352 had been NH. Still nobody home? He knocked again. There was a lace curtain over the window in the door. He could see nothing inside, but then there was a faint light and, after a bustle in the hall, the door opened. An old woman in a faded tartan shawl stood before him, and a strong smell of kerosene flooded from the porch. He hated the smell, which reminded him of his childhood and having to lug cans of kerosene from the tank in the basement of their house up the stairs to the big heater in the downstairs hall. Some of the oil would spill, and the stench never went away. His friends' homes had furnaces in the basement, and they had no fussing with oil. Now he too had central heating in his small apartment.

He introduced himself, in the way the campaign manager had advised all the new workers: "Madam, I'm campaigning for the Liberal Party for the upcoming election." Pause for a second or two then, he had been told, to pick up the tell-tale sign. No tell-tale sign was coming from the old woman, who seemed to be in another world.

"Come in," she said eventually.

In he went, through the porch and inside door, to a kind of parlour.

A kerosene stove was in evidence, together with a sofa, television set, table, and four chairs. There was no carpet on the floor, he noticed. Looking down, J.J. saw blood on his shoe. On the table lay a plate of meat and potatoes. There was only one setting. "Madam," he started again.

She stopped him, pointing to a box on the table. "Pick a card," she said. The box was full of what looked like playing cards standing on edge. "Always listen to what the voter says," Critch said at a workers' meeting, "and look interested. This is a potential Liberal in front of you." He glanced at the old woman again, who was looking at him with pitying eyes. "Go ahead, pick a card," she said. He picked one. On it was written:

> Thou shalt eat the labour of thine hands; happy shalt thou be, and
> it shall be well with thee; thy wife shall be as the fruitful vine, and
> thou shalt dwell in the house of the Lord forever.

J.J. looked at his hands: fingernails chewed almost to the cuticles, knuckles bitten and swollen. A carpet-fitter's hands.

He bumped into Critch next day at headquarters and mentioned the words on the card to him. The candidate said he would pay no attention to them. He had to hurry away because he was doing a TV spot in an hour. When J.J. told Dorcas about the episode a couple of days later, she laughed and said she was fruitful all right but she didn't look much like a vine.

Exchange of body fluids

Kimberley Manning lay naked in bed in the Hotel Newfoundland suite, waiting for her new lover to come out of the bathroom. She thought he was nice: an aircraft technician, well dressed, single, her own age. He'd do. This was her first time with him. She heard him gargle. What did he have in there? Listerine? He had already noisily brushed his teeth. Did he have gum disease? Would he floss next?

Henry Morton Robinson came to her mind again, as he had last year when she referred to the author of *The Cardinal* in an essay she wrote on the modern novel. She was doing university courses in the evenings for self-improvement. "Henry Morton Robinson!" her English instructor exclaimed, "Miss Manning, you are the last person on the planet to have read a book by that man." In fact, she had read not only Robinson, but A.J. Cronin, Lloyd C. Douglas, and a host of other Catholic writers whose works were sent to her as a child by a maiden aunt who wanted her to go into the convent. The books arrived faithfully every Christmas, interspersed with copies of the *Irish Messenger of the Sacred Heart*. Only Robinson stayed in her mind, because of a remark he had a character make about love. The cardinal's young sister had fallen in love with a Jewish boy named Iggy, but her horrified family talked her into giving him up and going out instead with a Catholic who chewed Sen Sen to keep his breath fresh. The heartsick girl commented, "When you love someone, you don't care how he tastes."

This observation had made an impression on Kimberley. As a youngster, she couldn't imagine that it was true. She wouldn't even drink out of a cup that one of her close friends had used. The thought of licking somebody else's spit sickened her. Spit tasted sour, she knew that. Her mother told her never to play the harmonica at school or blow on any of the wind instruments. Somebody with trench mouth might have used them the day before, and the only way to get rid of germs from spittle was by boiling. The germs could stay active for weeks. Kimberley thought it unlikely that the principal boiled the saxophones every evening, and as a consequence her musical education had not advanced on all fronts. She tried singing, however, and to her delight made the glee club. She would be able to sing "The Trout" to her children.

The bathroom door now closed and sounds from inside became muffled. What was he doing? She hoped there would be no smell afterwards. She didn't like the odour people left in bathrooms. Florient couldn't hide it, not really. She tended not to like male smells generally, certainly not ones from underarms or mouths. On her first date she had been taken for a drive by a quiet senior, a good catch, according to her mother. He was well behaved, when you considered what other boys were said to do in cars, but his breath had smelled of cabbage and his armpits, well, like vegetable soup. She could be quite precise about aromas. And when he made his move towards her after a little bit of talk, she could see a thin line of catsup in one corner of his mouth. She felt like vomiting then, and asked to be taken home. The boy telephoned her three or four more times, for she was a pretty brunette, much in demand. A bit on the skinny side, maybe. But she couldn't go out with him again. He ended up with one of the school cheerleaders, got her pregnant, and settled down eventually to a career as a lawyer. Now people were saying he'd soon be a partner in his firm. He really had been a good catch. Damn her eyes and nose, anyway! Other girls could put up with things. Why couldn't she?

Silence from the bathroom. The gentleman was performing; no question. Henry Morton Robinson came back to her. The cardinal's sister had been about her age. Kimberley was now twenty-seven, secretary to the manager of the Bank of Montreal on Churchill Square. She would rise as far as women could rise in the bank, one of the older tellers said to her. She hoped he was right. She was smart, and her mother said she had it in her to be an executive assistant at least. Kimberley understood business, she said. But last year Kimberley did a dumb thing — she fell in love with the assistant manager of one of their branches, Jeremy Dwyer, B.Comm. And he with her. It was the real thing, she knew it right away. But he was married and wouldn't leave his wife and children for her, not even after nearly a whole year. It was the old story. Kimberley said she had a door held open for him, but she couldn't hold it forever. "Take the door, Jeremy," she begged. But he wouldn't. "I'm the girl for you," she would say. She was, too. She waited until she saw the writing on the wall. Then she walked away. She had to. Pride, for one thing. People were beginning to talk. She needed security; her looks wouldn't last, her mother kept saying. And how much more could there be of necking in his office and sneaking off at lunchtime to cheap motels? Or of stealing into her house on mother's bingo nights? "Take me or leave me," she finally declared; and when, after many agonizing waits for deadlines to come and go, he said that he couldn't take her in the way she wanted, she dropped him. He had cried. He told her that what she was doing was wrong. "Love is a gift from God," he said, "don't throw it away." He said much more, for he was a word man. Argue! There was nobody like him. But she had her whole future to consider. "Give yourself a shake, girl"; this was her mother talking. She shook, all right.

What her passion for Jeremy taught her was that old Henry Morton Robinson was right about the taste of love. She now knew that not only were you not offended by the taste and smell of someone you really loved, you couldn't get enough of him. Jeremy's lips and tongue had a distinctive taste, but "give me more!" she whispered to him over and over as they lay together. AIDS be damned, she thought. She took his saliva into her mouth as if it were nectar, held it, savoured it, absorbed it into her being. She tasted his sweat and his tears; it was all greatly to her liking. She drank it in. "You're a taster," he said to her, "yes, and a smeller too." He was part of her body now, for she had digested him into her flesh and sinew.

To her great surprise, a skin problem on her back that she had been unable to cure for years disappeared when she started going out with Jeremy. "It's my bayman's juices!" he shouted one bingo night while frolicking on her bed, "I should bottle it and sell it to other townies with acne. All you St. John's people got dirty blood. It comes from being screwed for hundreds of years by European riff-raff down on the docks." What a tease he was; but she didn't mind what he said. He always made much of the fact that he came from Notre Dame Bay. And how completely he had swallowed her in return! Although he was mostly a hugger, she had made a taster out of him. She remembered, restless in the bed, how thoroughly he had made love to her. He hadn't learned that in Notre Dame Bay, she told him: "You had to come out from under the fish flakes to pick that up." He would laugh and dive back for more. She was part of him too. Yes, little sister of the cardinal, you were right, she thought, listening to the distant sound of flushing from the bathroom. Now her bozo — Jeremy called her other boy friends bozos — blew his nose. She cocked her ear for more. The electric shaver. Of course! He had to shave as well. His legs, probably. Men. Really.

"Screw love," she said at last when Jeremy failed for about the tenth time to meet one of her deadlines. "I've had it with love," she told him. "Who needs it?" There was a song that asked what love was. Was it a river, a razor, a hunger, or a flower? They would argue endlessly about this. She now thought it was a razor. And she meant it. The pillow was wet under her head. She would live without a razor in her gut, thank you very much.

The shaver stopped its buzzing, and she heard the door open. She could smell the Florient already. Oh God, she thought, cut back on the seeing, cut back on the smelling! Maybe it would be better now, after Jeremy. She had started praying again recently, but only because saying the "Hail Mary" about two hundred times in a row drove other thoughts from her mind and helped her get to sleep. A priest once told her that it didn't matter why you prayed; every prayer counted anyway. Looking towards the door, she saw her naked bozo approaching the bed. She chose not to look down, so she looked up at his face. It was a clean, good face. There wasn't much wrong with it. She couldn't see a bead of sweat anywhere. Kimberley swallowed hard and gently scratched her back where it had started to itch. Then she closed her eyes and got down to business.

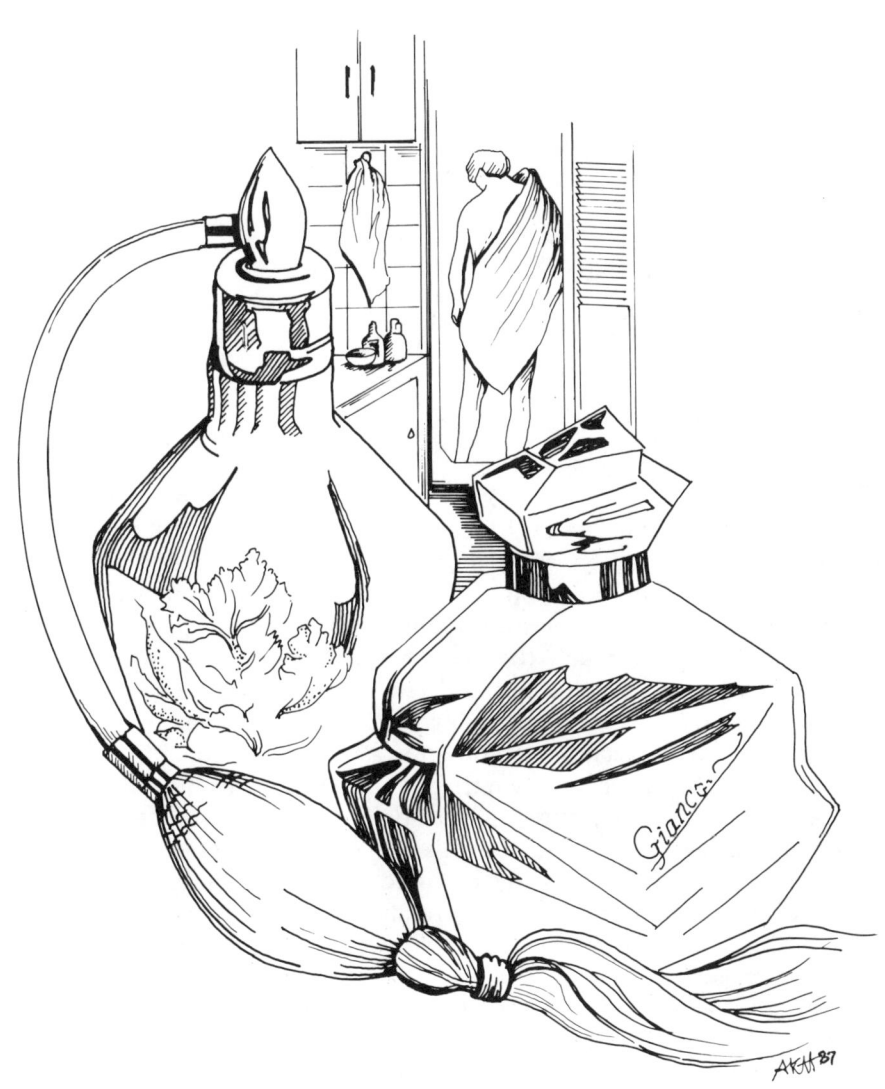

Leaving Anna

The rising young scholar, Anthony Fleming, first saw Anna Hogan in a path on Primrose Hill, N.W.3, in the spring of 1969. He was more than halfway through his sabbatical year and was writing a book, or so he told his friends, on Samuel Johnson. To be precise, he was attempting a new critical study of Johnson's writings. The project was not going well. He had made his way through the early works fairly quickly — they were imitative, conventional; he could understand those. But the deeper pieces of Johnson's middle years were giving him no end of trouble. Anthony read them again and again, searching for a lead. None was forthcoming. Something was happening in them that he couldn't understand. His progress having stalled, he would retreat almost daily with his sons, Thomas and Jonathan, aged six and four, from his flat on Eton Avenue to Primrose Hill park, a five minute walk away. He loved to stand on the top of Primrose Hill itself, the highest point in London, and look southward over the city. It gave him a sense of power. On a warm day in April near the hilltop, Jonathan chased his football, fell over it, scratched both knees, rubbed his face on the rough path, and screamed blue murder. He was helped to his feet before his father could get to the scene. The angel of mercy was Anna.

Anthony's initial impression was of her hands. They were big hands, with coarse, closely bitten nails and thick fingers. Some dirt remained under the bits of fingernail not yet chewed. A peasant's hands, he thought, and so indeed they were, for as he later discovered Anna was a farmer's daughter from Tullow near the Wicklow Mountains in Ireland and had been used to hard manual work from her earliest years. It was her hands, however, passing gently over Jonathan's bleeding knees and tearstained face, that comforted the victim. Taking a larger view of her as she held his child and rocked him, singing softly — strangely intimate behaviour with a little boy she hadn't even met — Anthony saw that she wasn't beautiful, wasn't his type at all. She was tallish, about his own height, with big bones and little flesh, flat-chested, tired looking. Her straight black hair, unadorned with ribbon or pin, hung down over her shoulders and, when she stooped forward, fell awkwardly over her face. Her thin lips had no lipstick. There was no eyeshadow, no perfume. She seemed to be totally unselfconscious — "the thing itself, unaccommodated woman," he would say later, to which she once replied, "I'm not much, but I am what I am." But he was North American, and in 1969 liked his women pretty and packaged. Taking Jonathan by the hand, he left the park and thought no more about her.

Two weeks later he met her again, walking one of her two children to school. It turned out that her boy, Michael, and his Thomas both went to Holy Rosary Elementary School on Haverstock Hill. She had been walking there with her son, as he had with his, for some seven months, yet he hadn't noticed her. She really didn't stand out in a crowded street. She had noticed him, she told him afterwards. On this second occasion, he was struck by her gentle way of speaking; they drank coffee together in a newly opened Espresso café, and he talked of his work. Quiet by nature, she let him ramble on about his efforts to grapple with the thought and style of Johnson — "one of the greatest writers who ever lived," he told her. Anna had only been to grade school and didn't understand such important things, she said; but she appeared to enjoy hearing him hold forth. He also spoke of his ambitions in the academic world. They had a second cup of coffee. Her eyes were brown, he noticed. She puffed cigarettes incessantly and so her breath, when he smelled it, was what could be expected from a heavy smoker. But he didn't dislike it, even though he hadn't smoked since he was a teenager.

At later meetings in the same café she told him of her life. She didn't rush to tell him; he had to ask. Her husband, an Englishman, was a clerk in Selfridge's in Oxford Street and had been in the same job for five years. Competition among workers in the department store was fierce, and there was little hope of early promotion. It would be another five or six years before they could afford a car. To make life a little easier, she looked after the block of flats she lived in and got a reduction in rent from the owner. She collected rent from the tenants, kept the halls clean, and let vacant flats after somebody moved. There was a lot to do sometimes, she had to admit. It was an ordinary life, she said, and she was satisfied with it. Her husband wasn't a drinker or gambler, and gave her no trouble. Once in a while he had too many pints on a Saturday night, but what man didn't? She would make sure her two boys were brought up right. When Anthony asked if she ever thought of going to the U.S. or Canada, she answered, "No." Monosyllabic answers were one of her specialities.

Back to Johnson he went, still hunting. "Did he have a wife?" Anna asked. Of course he did, but Anthony doubted if that fact alone had anything to do with Johnson's literary productions. Anthony Fleming (the name had already made its appearance in the learned journals) liked to separate the literary artifact from the maker of the artifact. He was a "new critic." He went on about this with such feeling that Anna raised her hand: "I didn't mean anything. I was only asking." But stuck as he was for a way to proceed, he now went over Johnson's relationship with his wife, Elizabeth Porter, whom her husband affectionately named Tetty or Tetsie. A widow of forty-six, Tetty had married the half blind and ugly Johnson when he was only twenty-six and had no prospects. Incredibly, it was a love match. David Garrick had been a pupil in Johnson's school just after the marriage and had watched the loving couple through a keyhole. Afterwards he would act out what he saw and heard as a party piece: Tetty lying in bed, waiting, hungry for love; clumsy Sam getting undressed quickly, saying, "I'm coming, Tetsie, I'm coming, my Tetsie." Garrick would have his audience roaring with laughter. Much of Johnson's life with Tetty during his years of writing remained obscure, though evidence suggested there had been stormy and bitter moments. He had left her alone for long periods to go on mysterious "rambles." But he had come back to her, full of remorse, and the intensity of the marriage had somehow been sustained. When she died in 1752 he was devastated. "Do not live away from me," he begged a friend who, having spent the entire night of her death praying with him and consoling him, had gone briefly to tend to his own affairs. Those who knew Sam and Tetty best, a contemporary biographer wrote, "wondered that Johnson could derive no comfort from the usual resources." Apparently not even prayer offered much help. Anthony himself found Johnson's response to her death surprising, in view of the writer's dedication to the life of the mind. Anna said simply, "He was crazy about her."

June came and went, and half of July. Anna and he spent more time together, though innocently: walking, talking, drinking coffee, often in the company of their children. Sometimes they met at Camden Town market where she went to get bargains. "You're important, Anthony," she said to him one day, "you're going to be a writer, a critic. Your name will be famous. I'm just a common person. Sometimes I don't feel right talking to you." He protested: "You're not ordinary, Anna." He loved saying the name. She turned away: "Yes, I'm a child-minder, flat-minder, man-minder. That's my destiny." He couldn't imagine such acceptance. She was twenty-seven, he thirty; their lives lay ahead of them. But she looked and behaved as if she were older. Her work was hard, but then so was his, he thought, remembering the typewriter with the blank sheet of paper. They had now started holding hands when the children ran off to the swings. He loved the feel of her big hands in his, though on closer inspection they were covered in little cuts and calluses. He wondered if she were telling him everything about her activities in the flats. How little he knew of the world she lived in! Once, carried away, he took her hands and kissed them.

In July he left with his family for a two week holiday on the continent, and when he returned she had gone to Ireland to her father's farm. A note informed him she would be back on August 15th. He was to leave for Canada on the first of September.

So Tetty died in 1752; but Johnson had known other deaths. Time was supposed to heal. Yet in the generally lighthearted and satiric *Idler* essays, written six years later, Anthony kept picking up the note of grief: "The loss of a friend upon whom the heart was fixed, to whom every wish and endeavour tended, is a state of dreary desolation in which the mind looks abroad impatient of itself, and finds nothing but emptiness and horror." In that essay Johnson was thinking primarily of his mother, but Anthony knew he had Tetty on his mind too. My God! he thought, how long does sorrow last? And guilt, what about that? He remembered that Johnson, in the closing years of his life, went alone to Uttoxeter market where he had disobeyed his bookseller father as a child, and stood in the rain, his head uncovered, while passers-by mocked him. That's how long guilt had lasted in him. What of passion? What was its term? Anthony thought of his own wife, Ellie, now busy pursuing her career at University College Hospital. Their holiday together had not been a success. He hadn't been able to eat or sleep. And what a lousy lover he had been. What was happening to him? Ellie had given him looks and dropped hints about saltpetre in the hotel food. He hoped she laid the blame on the slow progress of the book and the fatigue of travel.

A few days after Anna's return they met again in Camden Town market. A bruise showed under her right eye, but she didn't offer an explanation, and he was too alarmed to ask what had caused it. Though people were watching, he took her in his arms and kissed her lips for the first time. A shred of tobacco came from her tongue into his mouth, leaving a bitter taste. But he liked it. She was a perfect fit in his arms. He could smell her perspiration, and liked that too. She held him close, her hands lingering over his head and neck. "I love you, Anthony," she said. "Is there any hope for us?" Receiving no reply, she went on: "If you want me to come with you to Canada, I'll come." He didn't know what to say or do. "What, leave your husband and children for me?" he finally blurted out. "Yes," she answered.

Ten days later, sitting next to his wife on the plane, Anthony began writing: "What we see in the *Idler* is Johnson reaching beyond satire to a new form, a form that could accommodate both irony and love." It was the first time he would use that word in print, and he wondered what his colleagues would think of it. But at long last he had made a start on what would surely be an important critical article. He lay back in his seat, and the drone of the engines made him doze off. Jonathan and Thomas came tumbling down the aisle, pursued by a stewardess. Waking with a start, Anthony realized he had been dreaming of Uttoxeter market.

A *friend* to man

It seemed that the argument tonight was going to be on a new topic. That was fine and dandy with Marcella Foley. She was seventy years old and had had her fill of politics and religion for one summer. Her family seemed to be evenly divided into PCs and Liberals, Christians and pagans, and their Saturday night get-togethers to play cards had turned into humdingers. Mr. Peckford's ears must be burning for sure. One of her sons-in-law, Jim Flynn from Mulley's Cove, cursed the poor man last Saturday in language that you wouldn't use on a mongrel bitch. "Virgin Mother of God," Marcella whispered when he finished. When her Tory son Perce, the doctor, ventured to suggest that "the premier was doing his best," he was lathered with abuse by her mild-mannered son-in-law from Ferryland, Frank O'Brien. Usually nobody said boo to the doctor. He was taken aback. Marcella had to step in and steer the conversation back to auction. She had the five and jack of hearts and was ninety on game. There was a nice pot on the table. Jim Flynn, a poor hand at auction, had gone down seven times.

Peace and quiet was what she wanted. The sign in her front hall read: "Let me live in the house by the side of the road / And be a friend to man." That was her motto. Her family was reared and gone, and she and Ike only saw them during the holidays. Winters were lonely. She didn't want her summers spoiled by arguments. Sometimes she felt like making her two sons-in-law sign pledges to keep quiet before they came through the door. Not that they were as bad as her son Theo, the professor. There was no stopping him. He took the cake. Once he and his wife Nan even tackled Perce about the salaries paid to doctors. She preferred to forget all about that evening. Mind you, Perce was a complainer, and always felt doctors weren't getting enough from the government. "A doctor's fart stinks the same as mine," Theo said to him, "but when you fellows let one go you want to be paid for it."

The language! "You mind your tongue," Marcella said the next time she passed by his chair.

It was Theo who was now holding forth on the subject of marriage. She could hear him from the kitchen where she was getting the snack ready. "What is it," he was asking, "that makes us cling to the hoary practice of matrimony? Don't tell me it's a religious conviction about the sacraments. Or some notion that it's possible to love somebody forever. This is too secular and cynical an age for the old fictions." He was greeted by silence. If he hadn't mentioned and dismissed love as a possible answer, Marcella felt sure her daughter Cecily would have said it. She was still inclined to be romantic towards Frank. They had been married only three years. Nor did her religious daughter Lizzy say a word, though she and Jim were always first to the rails on Sunday morning. No one even remarked on the word whorey. Not nice, Marcella felt.

Normally she didn't care about the contents of arguments. She was only concerned that they didn't get out of hand. But this time, Theo got to her. What had kept herself and Ike together for forty-eight years? she asked herself as she cut the homemade bread into thin slices for the sandwiches. There had been many ups and downs. Hard times! She could tell a tale or two. When the youngsters talked about the disadvantages of Confederation she had to bite her tongue. But she had stuck it out — "punched it," as she often said. She had just done it, that was all. Thinking hadn't entered the picture.

She knew Theo wouldn't pause very long before he answered his own question. This was one of his tricks. You had to be smart to catch the little bugger. "No," he now said, "love and God have nothing to do with it. Marriage survives because men and woman have uses for it. Hold on, Mel, hear me out" — Marcella could hear Imelda, Perce's new wife from Ontario, try to butt in — "Wives are useful to men as cooks, waitresses, laundresses, housecleaners, social secretaries, accountants, child rearers, and handholders. They are also convenient alibis for failure and scapegoats for anger. When a man is stabbed, he needs a woman to bleed for him. She is also the receptacle of the sacred male seed and so provides dynastic assurances. And the woman satisfies a man's pride of ownership. Men need to own women. Look" — there was a pause, and glancing through the arch to the living room Marcella saw Theo set up his piece of theatre to clinch his argument — "look, this is my wallet, this is my watch, this is my Visa card, and this is my wife!" Nan was hauled to her feet and put on display. Theo would hear a few words about this when he got in the car to go home. Nan had a tongue in her too.

Marcella had to admit Theo was right. She had served those purposes. Ike couldn't boil water without burning it, she used to say. She had taken the bones out of her children's saltfish and sweetened their tea. To this day, when they came to visit she had to cut out and pass them their plates of dinner from the stove. She did that even on Mother's Day. The women did a little bit to help, but the men had to be waited on hand and foot. They were useless! On one of her tired days last summer she had wondered what would happen if she left the milk and sugar off the table or forgot to spoon the gravy on the fresh meat. But she hadn't tried it.

"Finally," Theo was saying, "wives are useful as ornaments to men, as indicators of success, or at least of wholesomeness, to the world at large. It is necessary for scoundrel businessmen to have some little woman at home whom they can say, or even think, they work for. Some men, from guilt, construct huge houses to place their darlings in while they go about their whoremastering. Thus wives are important to the construction industry and to the economy generally." This was said with a flourish. Theo had finished. For now. Although he said "finally," you couldn't trust him not to speak again. Both the doctor and Marcella's youngest son, Bram, the businessman, had built big houses for their wives. There could be trouble. Marcella hurried to get her blueberry grunt out of the oven.

Bram now got into the act. He was loud. Dark rum talking, Marcella thought. He took strong exception to what Theo said, and stressed the importance of marriage as a protection for children. Adults weren't important, he argued, only children were. Speaking for himself, he was soon going to quit the retail trade altogether and dedicate the rest of his life to advancing his children's careers in athletics. "If my boys want to ski," he said, "I'll go to the Gatineau Hills and buy a place so they can be near the slopes. If they want to swim, I'll go to Florida and buy a house with an Olympic-size swimming pool."

This was greeted with loud hoots from the assembled gathering and Marcella herself thought Bram's statements peculiar. As far as she knew, his two sons had never seen a ski, except on TV, and had never swum a stroke. Ike's old buck goat was more athletic than they were.

"You'll still be selling cabbage twenty years from now," Jim Flynn said to Bram.

Frank O'Brien added: "When your two boys get a couple of years older the less they'll see of you the better. They'll want their own friends, not some old cod like you hauling them over the Gatineau Hills." This thrust was applauded. Marcella cut the grunt into squares and wondered how

24

much her children cared for her. If Bram was an old cod at his age, what was she?

Bram's intervention having been disposed of, the main line of argument was resumed. "You must be wrong," Cecily said to Theo, "because women wouldn't put up with that kind of treatment. Who wants to be in a big house all by herself? Women have needs too. What's in it for them?"

Theo was ready with an answer. He always was. "In return," he said, "women get one of two things. If hubby goes on the bottle, goes off his head, or loses his job, she gets sanctity. It's nice to have the neighbours see that you're hanging in there when times are tough. And if hubby is a success, the wife escapes the responsibility of doing something with her own life. She can enjoy his status second-hand. So a long marriage makes a woman into a saint or a turnip."

Marcella grew turnips in her back garden. She was famous for her green thumb. Her orange lilies and bleeding hearts were the best on the shore. Thinking over what Theo said, she decided she would rather be a turnip than a saint, though she was renowned in the family for her devotion to St. Anne de Beaupré and St. Jude. She was a bit tired of sainthood. Now she wondered why Ike hadn't poked his nose into the discussion in the living room. Was he dozing off again? Wouldn't anyone notice she was here? Who'd stand up for her? She stood back from the table and surveyed the food. It was all there. The tea was steeping. She reached for the cups.

The lull in the conversation that followed Theo's latest revelation was interrupted by Imelda. "Speaking of saints, I have a proposition to make," she said. "This is such a wonderful family! Every summer we should have a special celebration in honour of someone we all love — granddad." Granddad was everybody's name for Ike.

"What about Mom?" Marcella heard Cecily whisper.

"Men come first," said Imelda. She didn't seem to care who was listening.

"Jesus, Mary, and Joseph, look down upon us in our time of trial," Marcella muttered to herself. She wished now she had saved some dogberries to put in the grunt. The cups and saucers were laid out, but they could damn well get their own spoons.

Mother Ireland

"It's hard to live with somebody who's perfect," Edie said to him on the way back to their hotel from early dinner in Limerick. He knew she only said that when she was really angry. Michael Fogarty, perfect? No, he had his faults, like everyone else. Meanness and nastiness weren't among them, however, and he replied calmly: "If you say so, dear." All he wanted was an hour or two in a real Irish country pub before getting on the plane tomorrow at Shannon. He had seen a promising one on a narrow road near Kilkee, and he had to go alone since he knew women wouldn't be welcome. So Edie would have to stay at the hotel with the children and wait for him. Was that a lot to ask? With a wife and three boys travelling with him, it wasn't easy to get a minute to himself.

Perfect: the word grated on him. It was true that people took to him, though. He was a likeable fellow. He recalled when he took his first job in Manitoba how Lennie Anderson and others in the department had warmed to him. It was from Lennie that he got the idea of a trip to Ireland. Lennie, the son of a Ukrainian immigrant, had once gone back to what he called "Mother Russia" to "reconnect with his roots." For months after his return, he sang Russian songs boisterously to all who would listen, drank vodka, and ate borscht. When Michael left for a new job in Newfoundland, Lennie was thinking of changing his name to Leonid Andreev. The writer of that name had inspired him, he said.

If Lennie could reconnect with Russia, why couldn't he with Ireland? He was a fifth generation Irish-Newfoundlander who, despite his education, somehow retained a strong trace of the accent and, he liked to think, a touch of the blarney. With a drop in, he could sing, dance, and yarn with the best of them. Of late years, he had grown proud of his Irishness, though he knew very well that to get ahead at the university you had to affect an English accent or, at the very least, be Anglican. But what matter! He would be true to himself. The three-week Irish trip in late summer, well planned by him for a year beforehand, was the result of this new-found interest.

The trip had gone well. They hired a car at Shannon airport and drove clockwise around the Republic, enjoying the scenery and drinking in the atmosphere. Edie found the daily quotient of "soft rain" a bother, and the children kept wanting to go shopping for models of tanks and soldiers, for they were at the stage when wargames were constant. But having boned up on Irish history and topography during the previous winter, he lectured his family daily on the glories of the countryside and the tragic story of Irish oppression at the hands of the English, not failing to draw the boys' attention to the fact that this was the land of their forefathers. In the Yeats country he read poetry aloud in the car while Edie drove. All were visibly moved. Near Oughterard in County Galway he actually located a "Fogarty Castle" and the family was duly photographed on the battlements. So the Fogarties had been kings! His most warlike son, Thomas, toppled a building stone from the side of the castle into the moat, somewhat to the dismay of the tour guide. Though the moat had long since lost its supply of water and was in fact full of debris, he heard the boy whisper, "Splash!"

This was but one awkward moment on the holiday. There had been a few others, involving, of course, the children and Edie, though perhaps he himself was partly responsible for the incident at Blarney Castle. He had looked forward for years to kissing the Blarney stone because he intended to go into politics in the near future and wanted, as he told Edie, "to augment his natural supply of eloquence." Up the dark circular staircase of the castle he bounded, followed closely by the boys, with Edie keeping well to the rear. The walkway to the Blarney stone was along the top of the narrow castle wall. A handrail three feet in height was all that protected him from a thirty foot drop to the pavement. "The Irish never cared much for safety," he chuckled to Edie afterwards. He walked gamely along the wall, as did the children. Son Jonathan had just finished spitting on the stone when Michael looked back to see Edie drop to her hands and knees about halfway along the walkway and begin crawling back towards the staircase. This caused some difficulty and not a little laughter, since people coming to kiss the stone behind them had to step over her. One man, rather a big fellow, trod on her hand. "Don't touch me," she hissed, when Michael approached to help. She crawled slowly down the steps, head first. Later in the car he explained to the boys the Greek derivation of the word for fear of heights. He rarely missed a chance to advance their education.

Edie sometimes got in trouble with the people they met in bars and hotels. He usually managed to find someone to talk to, and Edie would join in at first but soon grew tired of what she termed the "utter self-absorbtion" of the Irish. "If the second coming of Christ happened in Dublin," she said, "the 'troubles' would still be the top story in the papers next morning." Once in Dromoland Castle an Irish woman, after shaking hands, said sweetly to Edie, "You haven't a family have you? Your hands are soft, not like mine." "She's a bitch," Edie said to him in a whisper. For a minute he was worried she was going to say it out loud. He couldn't understand why she was upset, and he had to finish off her expensive steak dinner. But he kept the talk flowing and before the evening was over sang "I'se the b'y" to a full house. Lennie would have been proud of him. Afterwards, a man asked him where Newland was.

Making allowances for minor faults, he thought the Irish a wonderfully friendly people. The society seemed peaceful, despite reports to the contrary back home. He did notice quite a few graffiti directed at Americans; and soldiers were everywhere, on the watch for nineteen political prisoners who had broken out of Port Laoise prison. Their car had been searched twice, but he and his family were treated courteously. No doubt the soldiers recognized his accent.

Perhaps just one incident could be placed in the "distinctly unpleasant" category. At Sligo one Sunday morning the two oldest boys were sent off after Mass to buy comics while he and Edie waited with Stephen at a coffee bar. When the boys failed to return after an hour he went searching for them, only to find they had been beaten up by a gang of young hoodlums. He had been careful to have red maple leaves sewn on their jackets, and couldn't understand why this had happened. There was much crying and patching up, but little serious harm had been done, certainly not enough, in his view, to justify Edie's comment about an "undercurrent of violence" in Irish society. He strongly reproved the boys and told them to desist from fighting in future.

One special highlight of the visit was the climbing of Knochnarea, a hill near Sligo, to see Queen Maeve's tomb. From the top, over a thousand feet high, the view stretched for about ten miles. What a spot to drink in the mystique of Ireland! The boys, however, did not seem captivated by the vista. Jonathan said, "Why did we bother to climb up here, Dad? There's nothing here for us." Edie looked away. During the next half hour he had to restrain Thomas twice from rolling one of the big rocks on Maeve's tomb down the hill.

The holiday was over, save for the visit to the pub. After promising Edie to return within two hours, he set off and soon found himself in a small, smoky tavern where three or four men, possibly big farmers, were quietly drinking stout. Though he hated the taste of the stuff, he ordered a half pint and sat at the bar. He had hoped to hear some authentic music, perhaps a rendition of "The West's Awake," but there was nobody singing. It was still a bit early for him to try "The Kelligrews' Soiree." He had practised the song and was ready to perform if called on. Through the pub's dirty window he could see the bright Irish moon, doubtless shining now on lovers in Mooncoin and Tralee and on the mutinous Shannon waves. A television set in a corner blared about the Port Laoise escapees. They had not been located and a woman from West Meath was being interviewed on the matter. To her, they were "darlin' boys — they wouldn't hurt a hair on your head." He tried to strike up a conversation with the barman, but there was no response. After ten awkward minutes, an old man with a gaunt, weatherbeaten face entered and sat for a while staring at him. Michael waved his hand to the old gentleman, who seemed a touch under the weather, said "Hi," and smiled. He had a way of breaking the ice with strangers that Edie just couldn't match.

The man got up and staggered towards him. Thinking he was about to fall, Michael put out his hand to help. But the Irishman's face contorted with hatred. "Yankee," he said, and spat voluminously in his face.

Michael Fogarty wiped his cheek and took a drink of stout. Everyone in the bar was looking at him. The old fellow stood still, not three feet away, still glaring, unrepentant. "You fucking old turd," Michael said, and spat right back.

Edie was delighted to see him return so early, though she thought he looked as if he had been in a scuffle.

Mixed marriage

The incident at Witless Bay in the 1982 campaign perhaps could not be blamed entirely on his wife, but James Fahey was not inclined just to let her off the hook. If she hadn't cajoled him into taking her to the garden party and then, having gone, insisted on actually playing one of the damned games of chance while being pelted by rain in the school yard, the incident wouldn't have happened, and he wouldn't have lost — how many? Ten votes? Twenty? Not that it mattered in the end. He lost Ferryland district by twelve hundred votes. But it could have made a difference. How would she have felt if Damian Power's majority had been twelve instead of twelve hundred? These things happen. "This is politics we're in," he told her.

Talking over the episode later, he summed it up thus: "Evie, we're in a mixed marriage." To a third party this might have seemed a queer observation. In many ways they were a compatible couple. They were both Catholics of Irish ancestry; they were the same age, thirty-nine; they had the same friends, whom they had made while attending the same university and doing the same courses; and they shared many interests — music, theatre, literature. But he now regarded those as weak links. There were also deep differences of attitude and temperament between them, and these sprang, he now thought, from their greatly dissimilar backgrounds. She was from the St. John's middle class, and he was a small-propertied, raggedy-assed outport Newfoundlander who had made good. "A cute bayman," he had heard one of her relatives call him. Someone else in the family termed him "a bay-noddy." So he was. Their marriage embodied, he said, the townie/bayman conflict that pervaded life in the province. The conflict was a real one. Witless Bay showed how much trouble it could cause.

The more he thought about it, the wider he thought was the gap between them. It was a gap, really, in expectations. She had certain expectations of the world that he couldn't share. She thought it was rationally ordered, sequential, tidy. If she went to a supermarket to buy a pound of butter and found there was none, she would take certain steps that followed naturally from her presumption that supermarkets should have butter on their shelves. "Why don't you have butter?" she would ask, not a produce clerk or cashier, but the manager, no less. "And when do you expect to get some, please?" she would insist if, say, he replied that there was no butter. There had to be answers to such questions. The world worked; people whose job it was to get butter would find butter. James, by contrast, inured to scarcity as a child, expected there to be no butter on the shelves, and was always glad when he entered a shop to discover that there was indeed some left for him to buy. He bought it quickly because supplies might run out at any moment. Perhaps he might buy ten pounds of butter and pile them up in the fridge in anticipation of hard times ahead. Should the store clerk say, "My dear man, there is no butter for you," he would know this to be true and would offer not a word of protest.

It was the same in the area of movies. When Evie wished to go to the eight o'clock movie, she would delay the ten minute drive to the theatre until 7:45, knowing that a seat would be waiting for her that would offer a commanding view of the screen. He always wanted to go at seven o'clock, if not before. In his childhood, movies had been a rarity and when a Tom Mix film was advertised for the Orange Lodge in Burnt Point he and his friends went at 5:30 in the afternoon to await the blessed event. Then, if the man with the magic projector turned up from Trinity Bay, if the projector worked — how often he had trembled as the man tinkered with the projector, watching every expression on his face for a sign of hope — and if the electricity stayed on for the two hour duration of the serial and film, then, why then they would see it! But it was a dicey business. "Sorry, the projector broke," the man would sometimes say, "you can have your money back." He didn't want his money back. He wanted to see Lash Larue.

In something as simple as driving a car he could find illustrations of the divisions between them. Evie drove confidently, at the legal speed limit, without glancing to the right or left side of the street to see if children were preparing to leap out in front of her or if a drunk was staggering towards her some two hundred yards away. She drove on, knowing she would get through without incident. People didn't run out in front of cars. It wasn't done. He knew better, having been reared in a place where unpredictable horses, cows, sheep, goats, dogs, hens, urchins, and assorted other creatures used the road as a path or playground. He blew his horn at any sign of movement down the street, drove on the left to get as far away as possible from children on the right sidewalk, and kept his eye peeled for dogs and cops. If cops appeared they were surely coming after him. He would slow to a crawl. At a stop sign he wouldn't trust a car heading towards him with a right direction signal flickering. "Ha!" he would say to himself, "that driver is trying to deceive me into thinking he is going to turn right." He would wait until the car passed in front of him before he made his own move.

It was much the same even in matters of the heart. If Evie loved somebody, she said it and showed it. "I love you," she would say out loud to James early in the marriage, in front of his mother and father. He had to take her aside and say, "Don't say that." She also kissed and hugged in public. After knowing his parents for only a few years, she would enter their house and kiss them. This was a highly doubtful proceeding; it was, James thought, frowned on. Baymen didn't smooch or hug or paw one another. But in her family you came right out and said and did such things. And so you could, in St. John's; but not in Northern Bay, where he had grown up, or for that matter in Witless Bay.

The Witless Bay garden party was the climactic illustration of this tendency in his wife. Her view of outport garden parties was that people went to them to enjoy themselves. "They have to have fun sometimes, James," she pleaded. He explained to her at length that while there could be an occasional element of fun in such festivities for the outharbourmen, for visitors like themselves, a political candidate and his wife, there was none. A political candidate in rural Newfoundland, he said, goes to a garden party with a pocketful of $20 bills and proceeds to distribute them. He walks through the dusty, rocky school yards on which these events are held, and eats salmonella salad, for which he pays $20. He gives $20 to the priest; $20 to the town drunk; $20 to the driver who didn't get paid by the party in the last election; $20 to the inside agent who also didn't get paid in the last election; $20 to the local *artiste* for the replica of Eskimo snowshoes; $20 for a set of towels to the Legion of Mary; $20 for a case of beer to pass out to the local party executive. An outport garden party, he told Evie, is the twentieth century equivalent of the scourging of Jesus.

But she thought differently, and in Witless Bay proceeded to move away from his side and play the $1 wheel-of-fortune. This was innocent fun, the kind of thing one did at garden parties. It was raining hard. The man in charge of the wheel was wearing a necktie but no shirt. She won. $34 worth of tickets had been purchased, so Evie won $17, the other half going to the church.

"Look, James!" she shouted gleefully in his direction, holding the money up high.

He was talking to the priest about getting water and sewer in the parish hall. The government had already installed it in the church and parish house. He said calmly, "Play it again, dear. Use your winnings."

"All of it?" she asked.

He gave her a steely look: "Yes." He turned back to the priest for more important discussions. Soon he heard an intake of breath from the vicinity of the wheel.

"I won again, James," she said, again rather loudly. This time her prize was $46.

The priest was now giving him an odd look and he trusted matters were not getting out of hand. "She's got the luck of the Irish, Father," he said, "her maiden name is Kelly." This news seemed to make little impression on the cleric.

A small crowd now gathered around Evie, whispering. She clutched her $1 bills. "Shall I go again, darling?" she asked him.

"If you wish, my sweet," he answered, sensing the silent resentment of the priest. People were realizing where the real action was, and it took the man with the necktie more than five minutes to sell the tickets and take all the cash, even though the price of a ticket had been raised to $2. Conversation with the reverend father on topics of the day was beginning to resume when James heard the click of the wheel. Thank God! He would soon be able to get out of here. He was wet through. The priest's collar was soggy. Was it made of cardboard? The wheel stopped. She won again: $178.

A deathlike silence fell over the crowd. The prospect of a politician, even a would-be politician, escaping from a garden party with more money in his pocket than when he came was too much for them. Some edged away, muttering about greedy townies. "That fucker already got more money than he knows what to do with," one fellow said. James noticed the anger was directed at him, not Evie. There was only one thing to be done. He didn't dare risk advising Evie to play another game: he could see himself going back to town with a mortgage on the church. Before too many prospective voters for his party had left the scene, he retrieved the $178 from Evie's purse and presented it to the priest. "For the new sanctuary lamp, Father," he said reverently. The priest didn't seem to be impressed with this show of largesse, but he pocketed the money.

"Piss on him," Evie said on the way home, after he had changed a muddy flat tire on their old Volkswagen, "he's only got one vote anyway." James explained to her the nature of priestly influence over voters in the outports. "That's not the way it should be," she replied. He smiled. Seeing a bull in a nearby field, he blew his horn. Then he said he loved her. To himself, of course.

Now for the dance

He still had trouble with certain words. Not with spelling them or understanding what they meant and how to use them, but just with saying them. In the middle of what could be quite a reasonable attempt at discourse, he would stumble. Maybe it was his distant bog Irish ancestry coming back to haunt him. He recalled that once as an undergraduate he had been close to winning a debate on the history of capitalism when he said the word "mer**cant**ilism," and it provoked such laughter in the audience that he had lost his edge and become flustered. Years later, in a postgraduate seminar at the University of London, the professor of medieval English literature had asked: "Who here knows the name of the Icelandic scholar who rediscovered the manuscript of *Beowulf*?" Of course he had known; it was Grimur Thorkelin. Once he realized that no other student in the room had the answer, he blurted out "Thor**keel**in, Sir." "The accent, my dear boy, is on the first syllable. It is **Thork**elin, not, ah, whatever it was you said," said Professor Arthur Smith amiably. Tim O'Reilly knew that his *faux pas* would not be quickly forgotten. Stories would be still circulating about him in the Senior Common Room. "Had a chap here from the colonies a few years back, fellow named Reilly — or was it Keilly? — no matter — who said Thor**keel**in found the *Beowulf* manuscript," Smith would say. Loud snorts of laughter would follow. "Asshole," he had said to himself after the seminar, walking to the tube station.

Ten years later, now a professor of English and, for the past nine months, a member of the board of directors of the Canada Council, he was still wary of using certain words. For some reason words ending in *er* were starting to cause him grief: for "mister" he either said "mistah," slipping over the final syllable as if he were a cottonpicker from Mississippi, or else "mister," emphasizing the syllable in such a way as to create a ludicrous effect of a different kind. When he did a piece for the CBC nowadays, he took out all the words ending in *er* before going on the air. Finding substitutes for such words could be damned tricky. And words ending in *air* were also giving him trouble, though for years he had them down pat: "fair," for example, he often inexplicably pronounced "fayer." Just a few days ago he noticed as well that "here" was coming out "hair." He felt as if he should consult a speech therapist. But he didn't.

He brooded on all this as the quarterly meeting of the Canada Council was drawing to a close. It was the third one he had attended, and so far he hadn't dared make an intervention. He just didn't want to make a fool of himself in front of thirty or forty experts in the nomenclature of the arts. There were words he'd make a mess of, for sure. He just knew it. How could he avoid "mister," for instance, among so many Ottawa bureaucrats? Anyway, the meeting would soon be over and he'd be on a plane to St. John's.

"Now for the dance," said the chairman of the Council, Harold Heath. Art, music, video and literature had been dealt with in the morning session; it only remained to dish out money to the big ballet companies. All three wanted a ten percent increase in their operating budgets. In addition, towards the end of the blue book that contained the submissions from the "big three" were requests from two small dance troupes amounting to a mere $5000. Once this business was dealt with, Council members could head home.

"These are very carefully presented submissions, Mr. Chairman," said historian Jim Milbourn, the Council member from Toronto. "The three companies appear to have operated in 1982-83 with scrupulous attention to financial restraint, as we requested, and at the same time have kept a careful eye on quality. I heartily endorse their requests for a substantial increase in base funding, and I hope and pray that my colleagues sitting around the table will think as I do. But before I finish, may I say how grateful I am, we all are, if I can be so bold as to speak for everyone — and I don't see anyone objecting — how very grateful we all are to the Council's staff for providing such detailed supporting information to help us arrive at a decision, and for doing it in such a way as to make this difficult area of arts administration comprehensible, even to those not, as it were, in the know. It is a masterful job, and I repeat that the staff is to be commended. Even those who have come only recently to the Council" — Tim thought the venerable historian glanced in his direction — "can't help but be impressed. I think the minutes should record our appreciation." This was greeted by "hear, hear!" from two or three members seated at the semi-circular table at which final budgets for arts organizations were approved.

"Watch Milbourn, and learn," Heath told Tim when he took his place as the representative from Newfoundland. Tim had already seen old Milbourn operate in some tricky situations at Council meetings; he always got his way. An imposing figure, well connected in both the arts and politics, with white hair, thick glasses and a voice that rang with authority, Milbourn spoke only at certain strategic times and with the consummate skill that came from decades of serving on important committees. He gave the appearance of being a busy man, much in demand. Messages would be slipped to him by Council secretaries who tiptoed into the chamber while discussions were underway, and he would rise, excuse himself, and go off to make phone calls in anterooms. Tim would see him in the distance on the phone, making passionate points no doubt to the prime minister or his publisher in London. On returning after lunch to begin the afternoon session, the sage would often doze off, but in such a way that if you weren't looking closely you might think he was deep in reflection on a thorny point of cultural policy.

Arnold Safeway spoke next. Boy, they've got the big guns out for the ballet companies, Tim thought. Arnold was one of the corporate executives appointed to the board by the feds to ensure that fiscal responsibility would prevail in the Council's operations. He owned a chain of supermarkets in Montreal and rumour had it that he was worth a cool $30 million. His speeches were full of phrases such as "bottom line," "corporate plan," and even "merchandise." He tended to be gruff and to the point: you heard from him the plain talk of a man with far more important matters on his mind than the state of the arts in Canada. He attended only every second Council meeting. "Let's give the three companies the money they want," he said, "to preserve both their excellence and their international reputation. But frankly, Mr. Chairman, I don't see why the little folk groups from Nova Scotia and Saskatchewan listed in the back of the book need $5000. I think we could make savings there. It's not a lot, but we do have a bottom line, and a buck's a buck."

Next on the list of speakers was Sylvia Peso, a former ballerina who had had a hand in the founding of the National Ballet some decades ago. The trace of a cultivated English accent lingered in her voice, overriding what Tim thought was a hint of cockney. "I would like to add, Mr. Chairman," she said, "how much I too appreciate the efforts of our excellent staff, especially those in the Dance Section (she pronounced dance "dawnce"), but also how much I value the support shown by the previous speakers for the National Ballet and the other two companies. These are the country's national treasures, and no effort should be spared on our

part (she said "pawt") as they continue to enhance ("enhawnce") their reputation overseas. Our ballet companies must continue to get international exposure; the world must get to know them, and travel costs a lot of money." She now paused briefly. "May I also add just a word about the submissions of the Maritime and Saskatchewan troupes. I support what Mr. Safeway has said on that matter. Regrettably, Mr. Chairman, and I say this with genuine sorrow" — Tim noticed a look of pain on her face — "these troupes are sadly lacking in artistic quality, and I can't see at this point that there is any justification for awarding them the $5000 they want. It would take much more than that to create good dance in places like Nova Scotia, Saskatchewan and Newfoundland." She pronounced it New**found**land.

Norman Lighthead, the B.C. member who sat at Tim's left, turned to him and whispered, "No ballet in the boonies, old cock." This was greeted with laughter by Tim's neighbour on the right, a wily but companionable woman from Manitoba named Mickey Hewlett. "Ballet in Newfie!" she said. "That's a joke. You can't dance in long rubbers!" "Not leaky ones, anyway," said Norman. Tim grinned. He took a lot of ribbing as a Newfoundlander. "Order, please," said the chairman.

The stage was now taken by the representative from Northern Ontario, Sherry Sampson, an English professor who made a practice of promoting the interests of Eskimos and Indians. She had even been made an honorary Indian chief at a recent Ojibway ceremony. Tim thought she might well have defended the Maritimers, but she started on her usual spiel. "Plato, Mr. Chairman," she said, "emphasized form as the essence of things, the spume of ideas; but I am an Artistotelian. To my way of thinking, form must be melded with matter to create truth, the true thing, the object we call art. I repeat, I am an Aristotelian; we must not have just the skeleton of form, but flesh on the skeleton, if I can say that. Only then do we have art. Let me put this another way...." Tim knew she would expand on this for five or ten minutes. Looking to his left and right, he saw eyes glaze over and members slip down in their seats, pretending to consult the blue book. One or two put on the headsets supplied for simultaneous translation. Arnold was looking at his watch.

No good dancing in Newfoundland! Tim slipped back forty years to a cold night just before Christmas in the old family house in Long Beach. The tree was up, there was cake on the table, and he could have all the syrup he wanted. Since the rest of the house was cold, all members of the family clustered around the woodstove in the kitchen. What excitement! He was playing snakes and ladders with his brothers when his uncles came in, unannounced, from up the shore, to visit their sister: Gus and Eddy Hogan, with two friends, one of them a girl from Smooth Cove whom Eddy was courting. Their faces were red from the cold, and their overshoes covered in snow. "Come on in, Eddy, give us a dance," his father said. Off came the overcoats, off the gaiters, and out came the accordion. Gus played and Uncle Eddy stepdanced, for their pleasure and to entrance the girl he loved. Oh, how he danced on the kitchen floor that dark, cold night, shaking the funnel of the stove, rattling the cups in the dresser, sweating profusely in his ecstasy! "Give it to 'er, Eddy b'y," someone would shout. Sometimes he winked at Tim, and sometimes (though Tim resented this) at his brothers. His shiny black shoes twinkled; Gus played on. Eddy swung each leg up and clapped his hands under; all the family clapped too, even their grandmother. Eddy turned his heels up and looked behind as if to see that his shoes were properly soled; he playfully slumped forward, letting his arms dangle close to the floor, laughing as the feet kept tapping behind. Tim's mother beamed. Out came the home brew from the keg behind the stove. All but the children had some. Eddy drank deeply, took off his jacket, and stepped out again. Off came his tie, his shirt sleeves were rolled up, his shirt tails were out. He danced and danced; and in his magic feet shadowy generations of downtrodden Irish men and women from the farmhouses of Youghal, the narrow streets of Kilkenny, and the banks of the River Suir danced also. And their descendants in the forgotten outharbours of Newfoundland? Yes, these too darkly came forward and stepped out in his beloved Uncle Eddy's dancing, within that warm room of a cold house.

Tim's uncle, Eddy Hogan, could dance. And if the uncle could dance, the nephew could talk.

Professor Sampson now finished her oration and the time had come to vote. "I take it," said Heath, "that the $4.3 million requested by the major ballet companies is approved, but that the $5000 for the troupes in Nova Scotia and Saskatchewan, which belong rather to folklore than to art proper, is not?" This was a question. Tim noticed widespread nodding around the table. Milbourn said loudly: "Come on. Let's do it." Even the Aristotelian chief nodded. No voice of protest was raised. "Can we then move on to a couple of items of other business?" Heath asked. "Our time is getting short. People have planes to catch." Again there was a lot of nodding. The gavel was about to fall to confirm official approval for the major dance funding when Tim put up his hand. "Mr. Reilly, you wish to say something?" asked Heath.

"Yes, I do," said Tim.

"On an item of new business, or on the dance?"

"On the dance, Mistah Chayerman," said Tim, "I'm afraid we're deadlocked."

Then he started.

Fish killer

After looking through the binoculars, John Foley told his father there was something wrong with their net on Little Bank. Early this morning they had taken their best net from Salvage Point and moved it well out in the bay. It would be much harder work handling the twine and heavy gear in deep water, and nobody had ever tried to catch salmon so far out before. But why not try a new idea for once? John's argument had carried the day. "You'll get no salmon out there," one of the men on the wharf said when they came in.

Little Bank had been one of Abe Foley's berths in his great days of cod fishing. John recalled his father's precise naming of the marks for the shoal: to the north, Peg's Tolt between the spires of Northern Bay church; to the west, the top of the spire of Broad Cove church in line with the "man" on Western Bay Point. The churches had a lot to do with finding directions in the old days. There were plans afoot to take down the tall spire of Broad Cove church and his father would have to look for another mark up the shore for Little Bank. John knew he didn't like having to find new marks.

It was clear that the net, put out with so much care only six hours ago, was damaged. Only one of the two floats was visible, and the red corks that would normally be in a neat line keeping the twine and lead rope afloat were clustered together at the outside end. Had a longliner hit it? John had heard that some of the owners of big boats weren't as careful as they should be near salmon nets. Had the tide torn it? Had a piece of ice gone through it? It was astonishing how many accidents could befall a net in the open ocean. Overnight, a clean, new net could be transformed into a filthy, tangled object, full of holes. There was so much garbage in the bay that it was impossible to keep nets clean for more than one or two days. Mattresses, carcasses of dead animals, plastic bottles, old fence posts, and pieces of rope got snagged in the meshes. These were in addition to the normal refuse of the sea. On one occasion they had pulled sixty-five dead gannets from one net. All such debris had to be taken ashore and dumped; otherwise it might turn up again when the tide changed. Seals were also a curse to fishermen, and there was talk from other bays of finback whales and porpoises blundering into cod traps and ripping great holes. One do-gooder from the university wanted bells attached to traps to warn the mammals to stay away! The fishermen sometimes took grey seals ashore to show federal inspectors the long white worms carried as parasites by the animal. Three of the carcasses were now rotting on the wharf in Ochre Pit Cove.

There was nothing for it. Abe Foley would not leave a useless net in the water overnight. They would have to go out again today and fix it. Over lunch, John listened to his father hold forth on the mysterious ways of the Atlantic salmon. The colours of the salmon, Abe said, were given to it for protection. "Looking down, the back is blue like the salt water; looking up, the stomach is white like the sky. Who says there's no God?" Now seventy-five, Abe had once been the best fish killer on the shore. Stories were still told of him and his brother, John Joe, steaming down to Bay de Verde in their small skiff to go fishing on blustery fall days, while more careful men stayed ashore. They had anchored near Baccalieu Island at night and slept under the hatches in their oilclothes, sometimes on top of the fish. Only when the boat was full would Abe agree to come home. And he was still tough, though his legs had a touch of "rheumatic" and he couldn't jump around in the boat the way he used to because of his weight. But his arms were as powerful as ever, and sixty-five years of hauling rope and trawls had given him a grip of iron. To judge from the way he talked, it hadn't occurred to him that his day was over. John knew it was. He felt it was his responsibility to raise this grim topic with his father; he just hadn't been able to do it. Perhaps he was waiting for the right moment. Men had been overheard on the wharf grumbling about their small boat taking up space needed for the longliners. "Time for him to make his soul," one fellow said, not bothering to keep his voice low. Abe was hard of hearing.

After lunch they drove to Ochre Pit Cove and hauled their boat in to the wharf on a pulley system devised by his father and now widely copied. After stiffly getting on board, Abe took his bucket of twine needles, knives, and other equipment to the bow and stored it away carefully. The needles would be full, John knew, the compass dry, and the knives as sharp as razor blades. Throughout his childhood, John had watched his father gut and split fish with lightning speed and great precision. His own adult life had been spent in cities, but he felt no qualms about tearing out the guts of cod still trembling with life. He was proud of this rural capacity to kill, even if it didn't stretch far beyond fish. It put him a cut above many of his softened colleagues at the university. "We raise our bloody hands in pride together," he once wrote of Newfoundlanders in response to agitators against the seal hunt. His father, of course, had slaughtered many other animals besides fish in the course of raising his family. Shedding blood was as natural to him as harvesting turnips.

They decided to have a look at all their other nets before going out to Little Bank. Only six salmon were netted this morning, but two were over ten pounds and there could well be a new run of the fish starting up the bay. The net at Great Head, however, showed nothing but three sculpins and plenty of kelp. The sculpins were duly hauled on board, viciously "softened" by his father on the gunwale with a special stick, and then extricated from the meshes. Sculpins had to be softened; otherwise time would be wasted getting them out of the net and there was the risk of being stabbed by the thorns. Even Abe was stabbed on occasion. His curses on sculpins and other nuisances such as lumpfish were legendary in the family.

At Western Bay Point, where the tides were fierce, their net was half underwater and nothing remotely fishlike was in evidence. John proceeded to Swiles' Head where this morning they had caught two salmon. The silvery sheen of the fish in the water on approaching a net was a wonder to him still. But there was nothing in the net this time. On to Blubber Cove, Redlands, Isaac's Cove, Nelly's Ledge, the Barber's Pole, and Northern Bay Head — good spots when his father had gone back to salmon fishing seven years ago, but now crowded with gear and unproductive. When the cod fishermen saw there was money to be made in salmon they applied for licences too. All hands were chasing the elusive fish.

Their catch on this trip was certainly a meagre one: not a single salmon, six sculpins, three small codfish infected with seal worms and four pieces of driftwood. "Harvest from the deep!" John muttered as the boat headed at full speed for Little Bank. Cold and tired as he was, he had to stay alert because he was handling the outboard. Snagging the propellor in the open sea could be serious, though his father had spare parts and tools for the motor in his bucket.

A ten minute steam took them to the distant net. At first they couldn't see what was amiss; but when the engine was switched off they heard the laboured hissing of breath and knew they had caught a whale. Sculling closer to the outside buoy, they saw it was a large porpoise, six or seven feet long. The animal had struck the net in the middle, tangled its flukes in the lead rope, and torn thirty fathoms of twine behind it as it headed towards the open sea. Apparently it then tried to dive, spun around the outside grapnel's mooring, and came back up thoroughly wrapped in half the net. The net was destroyed. The whale's blowhole had fortunately turned upwards and in the swell of the ocean appeared above the water just long enough to give it air. It was barely alive. The porpoise had fought hard and the net had made deep cuts around the mouth and flippers. Blood was everywhere. It seemed to John to be coming from the blowhole too. Through the dusky water, about three fathoms down in a torn shred of netting under the whale, they could just glimpse a large salmon, twisting and turning in its own death struggle. It could weigh twenty or thirty pounds. In the circumstances there was a real danger of losing it.

Abe took a knife from his bucket. "Son of a bitch," he said. It had been a long day. Now this!

Seeing what he was about to do, John came forward, put his hand on his father's arm, and said, "Let's cut him loose, Dad."

It took half an hour. The blood soaked through their sweaters to their arms and chests. John got it on his face as well. It was delicate work cutting away the twine while taking care not to damage the animal further. Once freed, the wounded whale stayed on the surface near the boat for five minutes. Then it swam slowly away and disappeared. When they looked for the salmon, they found that it too had vanished.

The weather turned cold as they pulled the grapnels and the remains of the net into the boat. On their way in, the sea became choppy and John thought he might get seasick. Old Abe Foley looked at his whitened son. "It's time for us to give this up," he said.

When they got back to the wharf, it was hard to find room to squeeze in among the big longliners.

An episode in middle life

"My curse is candour," Jennie announced one summer's day in the twentieth year of their marriage, and as soon as she said it Brian Clancy knew it was true. They were lying on the beach in Northern Bay, playing one of their new games — spotting the ineradicable flaws in their friends' characters. The game was called "Curses." Jennie had turned the game on herself and Brian recalled some of the times her openness had got them in trouble. Once, in Manitoba, they went to a reception at the home of the brilliant young Head of Anthropology, whose party piece was wheeling out his ancient grandmother and asking for estimates of her age. Approached early in the game, Brian said "Seventy-three." When Jennie was asked, she said brightly, "Ninety-seven?" This put a decided damper on proceedings as the old woman was only eighty-six.

"That guy's a comer," Brian said to her later in the car, "you were supposed to guess low."

"But she looked ninety-seven," Jennie replied. She was incorrigible.

The Head of Anthropology saw to it that they did not get invited to his split-level again, and the old lady died shortly afterwards. Brian wondered how often Jennie's honesty had affected his chances for promotion in the savage world of academe where no mistake was ever forgotten.

He related the incident to her now, chuckling softly as he talked. This habit tended to annoy her. It had not been a good summer for them. She turned over on her stomach and sized him up. Then she said abruptly, "And you're a hoarder."

"A what?" he asked, momentarily mistaking the word.

"A hoarder," she repeated loudly enough to get the interest of some picnickers fifty feet away. "You collect useless things, Brian, and hold them too close to your heart. That's your curse. And I don't mean just material things, either."

He was stung by the diagnosis and turned off his old transistor to be able to consider it in silence. It was true! His sons were off at college, but his house was still full of their medals, trophies, skates, and books that he hadn't been able to throw out. And he was forever picking up pennies, nickels, and even screws when he and Jennie were out walking. "People will think you're a bum," she would say, a remark that squared well with the way he dressed since he couldn't bear to part with old clothes and shoes. He grew attached to things. Over the years he had amassed scores of Newfoundland cultural artifacts. Boot jacks, mat racks, cape anns, twine needles, kerosene lamps, horse combs, powder horns, paintings, ballads, awls, gaffs, and such like were displayed on the walls throughout his house. When he tried to put a rather heavy cast net on a wall in the kitchen Jennie asked him if he was trying to change her new home into a fish store. "In cast net, out Jennie!" she threatened. But he persuaded her to let him put a spinning wheel in the front hall, although it sometimes interfered with guests when they had a dinner party. When a visiting youngster was stabbed by the spindle, Brian put a large fisherman's cork over the point for protection. Now he was attached to the cork.

"This place is like a museum," a visitor said only a week ago. Brian was pleased with the remark then, but now he wondered. Jennie called him "Mr. Newfoundland," sometimes within earshot of rivals in his department.

Was he an emotional hoarder too? He had to admit he was. He stored up grievances and bitter memories and let them fester inside. He had parcelled up the past and laid it on dusty mental shelves. Clinging to old connections, he was occasionally shocked when someone he had been friendly with ten or fifteen years ago hardly remembered him. "You're not important," Jennie told him in one of their spats, "Who'd remember you?" He also tended to grow too fond of people he saw daily or weekly in his normal routine: secretaries, receptionists, editors, for example. He fancied they were fond of him in return, but now that he thought about it they probably weren't. They might well think him a fool. He took these transient contacts too seriously. He had always stayed away from love affairs because he dreaded having to choose between Jennie and some other woman. He'd want to keep both.

It was the same with his reading. The authors he loved — Swift, Orwell, Hardy, Le Carré — were so deeply cherished that he read them over and over rather than turn to new books. His head was a mausoleum, damn it! Lying in the warm sun, he thought the time had come to make changes. Next week would be a good time to start airing out his musty soul. Jennie would be in Montreal until Saturday evening on a social work conference.

On Monday he looked around his house for things to jettison and decided to begin with his Newfoundland paintings. He had a collection of David Blackwood's sombre prints about the Newfoundland seal fishery arranged in sequence around his living room, set off by his cultural bric-à-brac. Looking at them with the cold eye of the discarder, he thought, how boring they are! how dark, dreary, and repetitive! He decided to get rid of his one Christopher Pratt as well — the straight lines and tamed sea now struck him as mechanical. Too much had been made of Christopher. After telephoning the gallery to arrange the sale, he took the six paintings down and stacked them near the front door. That left an Arch Williams and two Peter Bells still in the living room. He didn't much like the look of Bell's stuff any more. Too red. But that could wait.

Turning to the cultural pieces, he decided at once to have a garage sale on Saturday morning to dispose of all items. His sons' athletic gear could be sold at the same time. He placed an ad in the paper, picked up price tags at the hardware store, priced every item, and piled the pieces in the garage. Standing back to size up the clutter, he wondered why he had bothered to collect it. Most of it was junk. Even the spinning wheel seemed overpriced at $95. He marked it down to $75.

When he got up next morning the walls had an empty look. He found it appealing. But the bookshelves were still full and he thought he might as well combine the garage sale on Saturday with a book sale. He emptied the bookcases and stacked their contents on the garage floor with a sign: "Books — $2 each." Only his autographed copies of the *Dictionary of Newfoundland English* were marked higher: $2.50. To compensate for this, he marked Farley Mowat's books down to 50¢. Even that was too much for them. He then brought the bookcases out and pencilled on each the price of $10.

This was fun. After phoning his secretary to say he was sick, he drove his old jeep, for which he had a strong affection, to the nearest used car dealer and struck a deal for $800. By the usual marital fiction, he and Jennie each claimed ownership of one of the family vehicles, but really he had paid for both, and both were registered in his name. After sizing this up, he walked home and drove back to the lot with Jennie's BMW, which he sold for $3500. He was beginning to feel wealthy.

By Thursday he had sold his furniture, including all beds and dressing tables, the lawn mower, Bell's and Williams's paintings, the shed in his back garden, his VCR, which he had bought only two months ago to watch his favourite old movies, and his wife's fur coat. How he had loved her in that coat! "You're insane!" she said when he told her what he'd paid for it. He gave the rest of the clothes in the house to the Salvation Army. The English sheepdog he placed in the SPCA kennel. He tried to sell the remote-controlled garage door but could find no buyers among his neighbours.

On Saturday, though he woke up stiff from sleeping on the floor, he conducted the garage sale with a special vigour and ended up donating all unsold items, including Mowat's books, to the Church of Jesus Christ of Latter Day Saints. When he had a television set, he used to love watching their ads.

In the late afternoon he rented a car and headed for the airport. On his way he stopped at a realtor's office and put his house on the market. "For that price, sir," the salesman said, "I'll have a buyer by seven o'clock."

The plane from Montreal was an hour late, but he had nothing better to do so he waited. When at last he saw Jennie coming towards him in "Arrivals," with a loving smile on her face and her arms open, he sized her up carefully.

The prophet

It was a long drive to Marystown, but Llewellyn Costello always said he enjoyed being alone. He also knew from experience that if you laid your cigarettes and a bottle of pop in the seat beside you, and turned the radio on every half hour to catch the news, the time would fly by. The five hour trip would give him a chance to collect his thoughts for tonight's speech at the Burin Vocational School. Not that he needed much preparation. What he would talk about had been settled, but he felt he should add a twist or two. Xavier Fagan, the school principal, had already heard him speak on Newfoundland culture a year ago in Torbay, and he would be in the audience again tonight. So Lew didn't want to repeat himself word for word. When Xavier heard the speech he came up and issued the invitation right away. "Great stuff," he said. Lew was becoming well known for his speeches. "The best I've heard since Joey Smallwood," the priest at Ferryland said last winter, "You'll be the premier too one day." A nun also made a comment to him on that occasion: "A wonderful talk, doctor." Remembering with a flush of pleasure, Lew realized he had been in top form that evening.

At Ferryland he was given a large replica of a killick, made by a local craftsman, to take back to St. John's. There was now quite a trade in such artifacts in the outports. He asked one of the youngsters in the school to carry it to his car since he didn't want to be seen leaving with his attaché case in one hand and a killick in the other. "If you start to skid on your way back, skipper, heave out the anchor," the boy said. Brat. Lew was only forty-four, not yet old enough to be called a skipper. His house was beginning to fill up with these tokens of appreciation. In the past two years he had been given four sets of bookends, one made of multi-coloured beach rocks and birch junks, an ashtray made of a seashell sitting on top of another anchor, two heavy marble desk sets bearing the Newfoundland coat of arms, with ball point pens attached by brass chains, and one miniature handmade figurine of a horse dragging a sled. Doris had started giving the objects away as gifts, but he insisted that some be kept. The horse-drawn sled was a special favourite. He had been born and bred in an outport and prided himself on understanding rope, nails and horses.

The Trans-Canada Highway was clear sailing as far as Roaches' Line. This was the turnoff if you wanted to visit Mr. Smallwood, now out of office after more than twenty years as premier, but still a powerful figure in the party. Lew and his colleague, Frank Hitchen, had called on him last year to see what he thought of their plans for the party's policy convention. They had to wait two hours to get in to see him. Frank did the talking. They wanted the executive, he said, to invite to the conference representatives from every district, and not just merchants and teachers, but the toiling masses — fishermen, fishplant workers, miners, loggers, the unemployed and pensioners. These would come together and tell the party leaders what they wanted done for the welfare of the province. "It will be a great exercise in democracy," Frank said. He was quite animated.

Mr. Smallwood spoke hardly a word during Frank's presentation, but at the end, appearing to levitate on the balls of his feet, his face red with anger, he shouted, "Pissy little people! Pissy little people! What the fuck to they know about policy? I know what they'll say when they come in from Dunghole Tickle and Shithole Bight. They'll say (raising his voice to a roar) 'we wants dis, an' we wants dat.'" The two visitors were then ushered out.

Lew thought it a disgraceful performance. "No wonder he lost," he said, and Frank seemed to agree with this conclusion.

How differently Lew had pictured the Newfoundland people in his speech at Ferryland. He talked about the ballad "I'se the b'y" that night:

I'se the b'y that builds the boat,
I'se the b'y that sails her,
I'se the b'y that catches the fish,
And brings 'em home to Lizer.

"What mastery there is in that ballad," he said, "what pride and power, what knowledge! How much that b'y could do. He could build a boat. Think of it. How many of us here tonight can do that? He could sail her, too. Can we do that now? No, we have lost the skills of the old culture." He then took a drink of water to prepare the audience for the last line.

"And why did the b'y do all this, ladies and gentlemen, what motive, what inspiration, lay behind his skill and work? His inspiration was (pause) Lizer." The expected laughter came; and Lew proceeded to elaborate on the love of family and the essential place of women in the traditional Newfoundland culture.

At Whitbourne he picked up a hitchhiker to keep him company on the drive over the Isthmus of Avalon. This really could be a tiresome piece of road: empty of people and traffic, passing through a succession of barren hills, separated by marsh and scrub spruce. Frequently it was shrouded in fog and you had to crawl along to be safe. Lew sometimes picked up hitchhikers for sociological purposes. He would get clues for articles and lectures from the drifters who were on the road, in much the same way that Samuel Johnson got an insight about the advantages of studying the classics from a sculler at Temple Stairs on the Thames. But the hitchhiker today was not a promising specimen. He was, of all things, an Australian, travelling the world before beginning his training for the ministry in some fundamentalist sect. When he learned where Lew was heading, he said, "Okay, I'll get out at Goobies." He knew exactly where he was going. He would spend the night, he said, at the point he reached at ten o'clock. Like the lilies of the field, he would be provided for. Though he seemed uninterested in the state of the Newfoundland economy, Lew explained to him as they passed Come-by-Chance why the oil refinery had been shut down. At Goobies the young man offered to pay for his share of the gas, but Lew said his expenses were covered by the school. In fact, he always found a way to add a bit extra to his bills to pay for the time he spent driving.

Lew turned down the long boot of the Burin Peninsula, on a newly paved highway. The Member of Parliament for the district for many years had been an influential cabinet minister, and no expense had been spared to keep himself in office. But Lew couldn't get too angry because the minister in question was of the right party. Passing through Swift Current, he noted a chicken take-out. Another sign of progress, he thought with a smile. The road now swerved westward towards Fortune Bay through another bleak and forbidding landscape, before it swung south to Marystown. Landscape! It was more like a moonscape. Lew had once been persuaded by an enthusiastic home gardener of the agricultural and pastoral potential of Newfoundland and subsequently gave a couple of speeches on the subject. He even convinced Doris to try growing cucumbers and tomatoes in their backyard. Since they had no children, he thought she might need gardening to fill up her time. "Don't lay your speeches on me," she said after the failed attempt. "Next thing you'll be trying is sugar cane." Now, looking out at the glacial litter that stretched for miles on all sides, he too wondered. What a spot! Nothing could grow here. Yes, there were pitcher plants and wild irises. But only someone with an aesthetic sense could see beauty in these. He could see it, but could ordinary people be blamed for not seeing it? And what good was such beauty, anyway? "I don't want your maggoty fish," the Newfoundland ballad went, in an expression of revulsion for all the island had to offer. Lew understood the feeling. He occasionally thought his talents would be better used in Toronto or Ottawa. But the dean of his faculty, a young Englishman who had quickly risen to the top at the university, argued that what Lew was doing for Newfoundland and its culture was important. He had decided to stay the course; now he was probably too old to find another job.

A note was waiting for him when he reached the Motel Mortier at five o'clock and checked in. Xavier would pick him up at 7:30 and take him to the Vocational School. Could he look after himself until then? Lew rather enjoyed lying around in a motel room for a couple of hours, eating steak and fries for his supper, soaking up the atmosphere. "It juices me up for the speech," he told Doris, who rarely accompanied him on his trips. He made his ablutions, put his pants on a hanger to restore the crease, and switched on the TV. *As the World Turns* was on; he had noticed people watching it in the lobby. Lew hadn't seen the program for years, but though he had no trouble picking up the story line he just couldn't get interested. He thought again of his speech. He had a good mind to try the King Tut idea that he heard Mr. Smallwood use about ten years ago in a talk at Carbonear. He took out his index cards and scribbled a few more notes.

From bitter experience he now wrote his notes in large print. He never knew what kind of podium and lighting he would find at the auditoriums and banquet halls in the outharbours. Once, at Avondale, when he was just starting on the circuit, he was forced to stack cups one on top of the other to give himself a place to lay his cards. His eyes were starting to give him trouble, and the cards had to be fairly close to him. He couldn't hold them in his hand as he spoke. That looked funny, and besides Lew liked to gesticulate with both arms. It was part of his style. An old hand at the game now, he actually kept a portable podium in the trunk of his car in case no facilities at all were provided by the host. A friend made it for him out of a few pieces of plywood. Lew hoped he wouldn't have to use his podium tonight because getting it out of the car and setting it up could create awkwardness.

But when he asked Xavier, on his way to the school, about the facilities he was told simply, "No problem." Xavier was full of talk about Loto 649, on which he had won $85 the previous week. All the teachers were playing it, he said. When they arrived, Lew was introduced to the Tory member of the House of Assembly and the Catholic priest. "I'm looking forward to hearing you," said the priest. "Somebody told me you were another Peter

Cashin." Five minutes later Lew was onstage with various local notables and the graduation exercises began. He sometimes found his mind wandering in such situations, but he wanted to concentrate hard this time to see what the young people were studying. Occasionally the graduates would look at him as they crossed the stage and he would nod and smile. The marine engineers seemed a lively lot; one of the beauticians, a short trim girl with a bun of black hair, gave him, he thought, more than a passing glance. Something for later, perhaps. "Born to blush unseen," he wrote on a card.

After an hour, Lew was introduced. Xavier had told him he had a maximum of twenty minutes. "People can't take more than that," he said, "and there's a party after." Lew looked out at the restless crowd of about three hundred — a youngish lot, but he knew how to play them. He started off with a definition of culture, not the "refined variety" — he pronounced the words with a mock English accent, grimacing and getting a chuckle or two — but what he called "the people's definition." Culture, he said, "was what makes a people distinctive, a breed apart." He went on to claim that Newfoundlanders had been, still were, and could remain, "a special people," distinct from North Americans, resistant to assimilation. He waxed eloquently on this theme. And continued:

> Three days ago I visited a traditional Newfoundland outport kitchen, the centre of the home, filled with the bustle of children, dog on the mat, a cup of tea on the table, not a speck of dirt anywhere, a neighbour in for a cigarette and a chat. All of this was wholesome enough, you might think. But there, smack in the middle of the kitchen, was a huge coloured TV set and the family was watching, with rapt attention, *As the World Turns*.
>
> I have acknowledged the benefits we Newfoundlanders have received from the North American connection. The real scene I have just described epitomizes to me the disadvantages. Right in the heart of the Newfoundland home we find *As the World Turns*. I fear that, as much as I do the smoke stacks and the oil tankers and the pornographic films, and the other evidence of material prosperity. What effect such mindless vulgarity as that program is having on our culture and values can only be imagined. I have the strong suspicion that the effect is bad; that, if we are not careful, our sense of identity as a people may be eroded away and lost. We must take charge of our own culture and identity. We must! The purpose of education in Newfoundland must be, more and more, to remind young people of their roots; to give them knowledge of themselves and their communities; to ward off the horror of alienation, which is such a conspicuous feature of North American urban civilization.

He heard an "ahem" on stage, and wondered if he was using words that were too long. But when he glanced at Xavier he saw him raise two fingers. He had only two minutes left. Time for King Tut:

> King Tut's tomb was opened by archaeologists in 1924. Among its treasures, hidden from view for twenty-five centuries, were the things the young Pharaoh had thought most precious: much gold, of course, toys, his mother's hair, and a seed. Yes, a grain of seed; one grain, in a cup, by the body.
>
> The archaeologists took that seed and planted it; and though it had lain in the darkness of a grave for twenty-five long centuries, it took root. A flower grew, one not born to blush unseen.

Lew now made his right hand into a fist and held it high, letting it tremble. He had seen this done before, with telling effect. He finished:

> That's like the people of Newfoundland. For three hundred years we have been held in a kind of political and economic and cultural darkness. But an old seed has now been planted in new soil; and it will grow bountifully, for our children and our children's children, on this chosen spot of God's good earth.

He had wondered if God should be brought into it, but someone told him this was mainly a Catholic community and he thought the reference wouldn't be out of place. It seemed to work. The applause was vigorous.

Xavier got up, thanked him briefly, and presented him with a small token of appreciation from the teaching staff of the school: a miniature dory, about three feet in length, complete with painter, thole pins, and paddles. It was well done and suitably engraved where the name of the real dory might be found. Xavier then spent a few minutes saying where the party was, what band was playing, and how much he regretted that because of financial restraint in the school, which he hoped the government member present would take due note of, the bar would have to be a cash bar. At this there was much groaning and hissing.

Lew thought it was expected of him to put in an appearance at the party, and though he wasn't a drinking man, he went along to the cafeteria and moved from table to table. Once or twice he thought he picked up the smell of marijuana, but surely he was mistaken. After an hour he found himself sitting with the black-haired beautician who, to his suprise, was unescorted. "I go wherever I want," she explained, "sometimes with a man, sometimes not." Her name was Betty Turpin and she lived in Garnish, Fortune Bay, a fishing community he had never visited. "It's off the beaten track," she told him, "nobody important goes there." When the band played a slow tune Lew asked her to dance and she agreed, holding him close.

Her breath was sweet, her eyes lively. Back at the table, for some reason he talked a lot and brought the conversation around to his speech. "Get your head out of the books," she said abruptly, "join the real world." A young man wearing a gold necklace bounded over to them and dragged her off to dance to a loud, fast number. She seemed only too willing to go, and once on the floor was in no hurry to come back to the table. Lew sat alone, watching her laugh and move. She was quite beautiful, really. Graceful, too. He flushed with shame when he remembered his fantasies about her on stage. Her sweetness wouldn't be wasted. Enough of that nonsense! He thought of leaving his dory under the table, but that might create a fuss if a dancer called out to him to come back and get it. He took it under his arm, holding it carefully so the thole pins and paddles wouldn't fall out, and moved towards the exit sign. A group of marine engineers were drinking beer and playing darts near the door, and one of them shouted: "That's a good looking dory, old man, but I'd say she'll be a bit tricky in a breeze." The remark was greeted with a roar of laughter. He hoped Betty hadn't been looking in his direction. When he reached the motel, he was surprised to find that his eyes had filled with tears.

Tokens

Early Friday morning a loud knocking just outside his bedroom window woke him from his sleep. He glanced at the clock, whose illuminated red numbers were the only source of light in the room: 2:23 a.m. This was crazy! It was the second time this week it had happened. On Tuesday the knocking had come at 2:22 a.m. Once again his miniature schnauzer sleeping at the foot of the bed hadn't barked or stirred. The animal was so highly strung that it yelped frantically at any visitor or strange sound. It even barked at Jan when she came out on weekends. Bending forward in the darkness, he put his hand on the dog's warm body, twisted as usual into a tight circle. It gave a low growl of protest at being disturbed. Apparently it had heard nothing. Had he dreamt the knocks? His father and mother, who lived a few miles down the shore, told him he had. But they didn't want to talk about it. What he heard could be a token, they said. His father's brother, Patrick, had heard a knocking high on the outside wall of their house just before their own father's premature death in 1930. It was best not to discuss such things. He parents were both in their seventies. His mother still bounced around as if she were forty, but his father hated to talk of sickness and dying.

He was living in his cabin at Ochre Pit Cove where he had moved to spend the entire fall term alone. He had "earned" the time off from his university chores by taking on extra teaching during the past three years. He now made a practice of being on his own for extended periods. Jan had been angry at first when, at the age of forty-three, he insisted on having time to himself to write. She claimed it signalled a falling off in his love for her. But he allowed her to come every weekend and bring friends. She would turn up later today with Fred and Nancy Spence and their two children. Fred had decided to build a summer cottage near his. "I can't imagine why," Jan said, "you're antisocial. All the fun has gone out of your life." Jan's weekend visits were convenient for him really, as she would bring the mail from the university and the newspapers. Though he had lost interest in what was going on in his department, he felt a bit cut off from events. There were times he felt a twinge of interest and remorse. As for the guests, Jan said it was important for him to see people now and then. She thought something queer was happening to him.

After the knocking on Tuesday, he had taken the ladder out of the barn and inspected both his bedroom window and the steeply gabled roof. He tended to roll towards the side of the bed near the outer wall as he slept, and the ceiling at two o'clock in the morning was only about two or three feet above his head. Perhaps a bird had landed on the roof and struck it. He knew this was highly unlikely, but there had to be some explanation. Crows and gulls circled over his house all day long. The crows nested in a nearby grove, and cawed from dawn to sunset at farm animals, other birds, and occasional walkers who strayed near their domain. It was conceivable that some crisis had led to erratic behaviour. But when he carried out his investigation there was no sign of anything unusual on the shingles or clapboard. He wondered afterwards what he had imagined he would find, even if birds had landed there. Bill marks? Droppings? Was this Hitchcock's *The Birds* he was in? But before he dozed off he decided to have another look today.

Normally a brisk October morning would have restored his spirits a little, but he was in an irritable mood after his poor night's sleep and not even the bright red, yellow and brown colours of the low shrubs in the meadow across the lane made an impression on him. In climbing the ladder to conduct another futile examination of the roof and the boards around his window, he drove a large splinter deep into the palm of his right hand and it took half an hour to root it out with an old stocking needle he found in the pantry. In process he got blood all over his blue jeans. The hand would be sore for days. Spending four months here was going to be rough. He had passed his childhood on the shore and was inclined at times to romanticize it, but today it seemed drab and cold. Many of the houses in Ochre Pit Cove were summer cottages and were shut up now that the season was over. It was desolate here in the fall. The sea was forbidding; most of the fishermen had already given up for the year. From his kitchen window their overturned white boats on the edge of the cliff looked like a row of headstones. Wind was constant and there had already been a couple of snow showers. Through two hundred years of settlement hardly anybody on the bleak coast had prospered. On his walks in the neighbourhood of his cabin, he saw the marks of human failure: an abandoned railway track, furrowed grassland that had once been vegetable gardens, the crumbling foundations of root cellars, and clumps of birches and poplars planted decades ago in front of houses but growing now in silent mockery of the effort to make this wilderness homely. A few hundred yards inland from the cabin a local contractor was starting to dig a gravel pit in a big meadow that not too long ago had been used by residents as a dump for old cars. About fifty wrecks dotted the landscape, though they were not visible from the highway, and some passers-by still thought the place was pretty.

When Jan and the Spence family arrived in the early evening he delayed the inevitable card game as long as he could without seeming impolite. He hadn't had much success lately in auction or forty-fives. Every night of the past week he had played cards with his parents and hadn't won a game. It was embarrassing. He was an excellent auction player and was expected to win often. After losing two more games, he steered the conversation towards literary topics. To his annoyance, a large chunk from one of his best pieces had recently been reprinted without authorization and used out of context in one of Herbert W. Armstrong's fundamentalist Christian magazines. It was a descriptive article on the eight-four men who had perished in the sinking of the *Ocean Ranger* in 1982. The magazine had used the deaths of the men to point up the moral of "helpless modern man floundering in a whirlpool of sin and godlessness."

"I didn't intend any of that nonsense," he now told Fred. "The *Ocean Ranger* tragedy was just a human and engineering event, an isolated happening. It means nothing."

"It could mean something, if there's a God and a spirit world," Jan said, butting in. "You didn't invent the sinking, you only wrote about it. How do you know what it means?"

Seeing Jan tackle him, Fred too jumped into the fray. "It's just as arrogant to say it means nothing as to say it means x or y," he said.

Nancy said not a word, though he could see that she would, if she spoke, side with Jan and Fred. She was a big girl who sat back and smiled a lot. Sometimes he felt like hitting her.

He fought back. "If the ballast control operator on duty that night had known how to do his job the rig wouldn't have sunk, and the men wouldn't have died. It's that simple, folks. It's just human stupidity. We are all stupid a lot of the time," he continued, glancing at each of them in turn, "but we don't all control ballast valves on offshore drilling rigs and so do little harm as we live out our tiny lives."

"Some things that happen do have meaning outside themselves," Jan insisted. He groaned. The next thing she'd want would be to get him inside a church.

After lunch next day he and Fred set out up the shore to look at possible sites for summer homes. On the way they stopped at the doctor's clinic to get medicine for Fred's daughter, Tracy, who had the 'flu. The thought crossed his mind to have the doctor look at his hand, which was very sore and still seeping blood, but he decided against it. It was time for him to give up on doctors. Passing through Western Bay he saw a new highway sign pointing to Bradley's Cove, the site of an abandoned community about two miles off the road in the direction of the salt water. To get there you drove over a treeless hill that was simply a huge bald rock. Not that there was any special reason for going there. It was lifeless. Like the Banfields of Gusset's Cove and the Tricketts of Spout Cove, the Whelan and other families of Bradley's Cove had given up trying to scratch a living from their barren shore in the 1920s and '30s, and had fled to Boston. No doubt their descendants were blessing the day they had the good sense to get out. These coves were now used only as pastures and picnic sites. He had gone out to Bradley's Cove once or twice as a youngster in his father's truck. Vigorously courting, he remembered. The girl's name was Marie Kelloway. He wondered what became of her. She had been lively and beautiful.

The road out had fallen into such total disrepair that he thought he might have wandered off onto a cow path. Even in four-wheel drive, his jeep laboured over the rocks and through the deep mud holes. In gearing down he reopened the cut in his hand and he could feel the warm blood wetting the bandage. Halfway up the hill, about a mile from the nearest house in Western Bay, they came upon a woman, walking alone. "Ask her if we're on the right road," he said to Fred when they were about to pass her. He stopped the jeep and Fred rolled down the window. "Excuse me, is this the way to Bradley's Cove?" he asked. She came closer to the jeep; her face was deathly pale and he was startled to see a patch over her left eye. He couldn't recall anybody with such a patch living on the shore.

"You're on your way," she said, looking through the window, not at Fred but at him. "It's just up over the hill."

They drove on. He glanced through the rearview mirror and saw her walking up the road behind them. Did she have a limp? He thought she might, but the road was so rough under foot that he couldn't be sure.

Descending into Bradley's Cove he could see that not a house or barn was left of what had once been a large village. A few fences were maintained around meadowland where men from Western Bay kept their cattle, and there were rock walls and ruined concrete foundations at various places. In the course of a few decades most signs of human life had vanished. The garbage that was sprinkled here and there had been left by picnickers. Beer bottles had been smashed even on the road, and they were forced to stop the jeep a couple of times and kick large pieces of glass out of the ruts ahead to avoid flat tires. It was a dreary, lonely place. Fred quickly rejected any thought of building a summer home there, and they decided to head back up the hill towards home. As they got in the jeep they could see the woman in the distance, on top of the hill they had just come over. She had stopped walking and was staring in their direction.

But when, three or four minutes later, they got back to the hilltop, she was gone. No bush, rock, or crevasse was visible. It did not seem possible for her to hide from them, even if there were some conceivable reason for her to do so. Thinking she had fallen somewhere nearby, they got out of the jeep and carried out a brief search. There was no sign of her. There was nowhere for her to go. Yet she had disappeared. Fred said, "Let's get out of here."

"Hannah Mulley was born in Bradley's Cove and had a patch over her eye," his father told them that night when they made their usual Saturday jaunt down the shore to play cards. The story of Hannah and her young daughter was a familiar one. The two had gone berrypicking in late October about fifty years ago from their home in Burnt Point, where Hannah had moved after her marriage. They lost their way in a freak early snowstorm. Years later, their bodies were found under a hill — now called Hannah's Tolt — a distance inland from Ochre Pit Cove. They had walked six or seven miles in the wrong direction before lying down and giving up their struggle. Possibly the daughter had been unable to go farther. Hannah died with her child in her arms. There was another question he wanted to ask his father, but it would upset Jan if he brought it up. He let it pass.

The event at Bradley's Cove put a pall on their weekend and Jan and their two friends left early on Sunday afternoon for the city. Fred, he noticed, hadn't talked much during the morning about building a cabin near his. Yesterday he had been asking if there were any good carpenters left on the shore. Jan, too, wasn't her usual plucky self. "Oh, for Christ's sake, it was some woman who ducked off behind a rock," he said to her before she got in her car. "This is the twentieth century. There are no more goblins. What you see is what you get."

She seemed comforted by this display of his usual short temper. "You take care of yourself. Don't go back there. I love you," she said before she drove off.

He just waved and went into the house. That night he heard the knocking again, as he knew he would. He guessed what time it was before he looked at the clock.

He woke next morning with his hand and arm burning. He'd be damned if he's go to the doctor. The hand and wrist were now red from infection, and there was pus around the cut. He washed it in hot water, wrapped it in a clean bandage, and took six aspirins. Since he would need more later he put the bottle, still half full, in his pocket. There were chores that had to be done outside, including spreading manure on the patch of ground where this summer he had vainly tried to grow onions and carrots. Next year whoever tilled the ground might have more luck. In the late afternoon he drove down to his father's house and asked the question that had been on his mind on Saturday night. Yes, Hannah had limped, but only a little, his father told him.

On the way up the shore he drove past his own lane and headed back towards Bradley's Cove. The dog? Yes, there was that to think of, but he was past caring. His arm was aching so much that the pain brought tears to his eyes. Blood was trickling from the sodden bandage onto the floor of the jeep. And he would have to drive over that cursed road again! He turned off once more in Western Bay and went down the empty road towards the sea. The rocks and holes seemed bigger and deeper than they were on Saturday. He lurched forward, unafraid, into the twilight. As he neared the top of the hill he hit a patch of fog, and through it saw the two shadowy figures waiting for him.

Printed in Canada